CHRISTMAS LOVE
YEAR ROUND

BOOK 1 OF THE KINDRED LAKE SERIES

ELAINE STOCK

G†G

Publishing

Christmas Love Year Round by Elaine Stock

© 2018 Elaine Stock

Published by GTG Publishing

ISBN: 978-0-9995763-3-5

This novel is a work of fiction. Any mention of real events, businesses, organizations, and locales is intended to give the fiction a sense of reality. Names of characters, incidents, and dialogue are solely the product of the author's imagination and creativity and are not expected to be real. Any resemblance to actual persons, living or dead, is entirely coincidental.

Cover Design by SelfPubBookCovers.com/JAMILLER.

1

$\mathcal{T}$he chink of glass shattering zoomed upstairs. In her bedroom Cami Richardson jumped and brushed against the curio shelf lined with her favorite trinkets. Her great-aunt Fran's beloved ceramic and glass music box flew from her hands. She gasped as the antique box struck the corner of the bureau and shattered into countless pieces on the bare oak floor, mimicking the crash below. Big chunks. Small shards. No matter. Her son came first.

With a sprint worthy of any athlete's admiration, she barreled into the living room lit only by the setting sun. "Danny? Are you okay?"

"It's him, Mom." Eight-year-old Danny crouched on his knees before the picture window. He peered out between the cutout Christmas tree and snowmen stencils they'd decorated with earlier to add cheer to the otherwise gloomy November day.

"Who?" She craned her neck for a look over Danny's shoulder. The neighbors' houses all appeared the same. No apparent activity raised any suspicions, not that she expected trouble. The cluster of 1980s-built houses, modest brick and wood-shingle structures that whispered a silent welcome, sat on a maple-lined block. Both hard-working parents and retirees enjoyed and maintained its tranquility.

Danny shot her a quizzical look then returned to staring out the window. "It's the same guy I saw at Friends."

"I don't see anyone, hon." She switched on the lamp on the end table. The other lamp scattered in broken pieces on the living room floor evidently was the noise she'd heard minutes ago. She'd deal with the damage later.

"Oh, Mom. Now I can't see out."

She sat beside her son. "Let's calm down."

"I can't. He's looking at the house for sale."

"Lots of people have looked at that place. What's different about this man?"

Danny sank below the window ledge, bobbing up every few seconds for a glance.

"Hey, my candy kiss, tell me what's up."

Danny slid fully onto the sofa and tucked his feet under him. "I know it's him. He talked with the director. I was in the back room, so I don't think he saw me."

Cami wrapped an arm around her little boy. Her mind raced as she shifted through the possibilities at Friends. Modeled after the nationwide Big Brothers Big Sisters, the town's program provided an adult relationship to children in need of either an older sibling or parental figure. "Is he the one taking Owen's place?"

Danny nodded into her side. "That's what the director said, but you have to say yes."

Ah. It was making sense now. No big bad man.

"What's this person's name?"

Danny shrugged. "I forget."

"Owen had to move to Texas, hon."

"But I want him back. Texas is far from here."

At times, everywhere seemed far from Kindred Lake, Pennsylvania. Yet, for a woman who craved to forget her past, she'd chosen to live in her childhood town. Go figure!

"Owen was a nice Friend." She gently swept away the hair that had fallen across his eyes. "Remember, Owen's planning to phone once he settles down."

"Owen was the coolest. I don't want this new guy to be my Friend."

"Why not give it your best shot?"

"I don't want to."

She glanced at the mantel over the fireplace at the framed eight by ten photograph of her, Todd, and Danny taken at Cape Cod the summer before Todd died. Danny looked just like his dad with his sandy blond hair, blue eyes, and a matching dimple to the right of his mouth. Her precious reminder of Todd. She swallowed hard, pushing aside her own discomfort.

"He must be pretty awesome to want to be a Friend. And you know, buddy. The director only allows nice people to volunteer. It's like me at work. I choose only the best teachers for Little Bears."

"Really?"

"Absolutely. I take good care of my preschoolers, like the director at Friends looks out for all the girls and boys."

"Gavin. That's his name."

Her neck pinched. "Gavin?"

"Mom? You just made a weird face."

Gavin.

Definitely a strong, kind of enchanting name, but not common. She'd known one Gavin. Gavin Kinkaid. Funny how that name still propelled her down the old guilt trip road. This man couldn't have been the same person she'd graduated high school with fourteen years ago. Back then she was beyond thrilled they'd gone their separate ways. The relief he experienced must have transformed his whole world. She couldn't blame him.

She licked her lips. "Well, Gavin is certainly a nice name."

"No it's not, Mom. It's a dorky name. Not like Owen or Cooper or—"

Danny was beginning to recite the other adult Friends. She signaled for him to stop. "Gavin's a fine name too. Besides, it's not nice to judge a person." The contradiction between her just spoken words and her past actions twisted her heart. But she wanted to set a better example than the ones she had followed years ago. "Let's be nice to Gavin."

"Don't want to. I just want Owen back." Danny squirmed loose of her hold and slid off the sofa. "I'll be right back. Got to get something from my room." He trotted upstairs.

With her curiosity getting the best of her, she couldn't help but glance out the window. The for-sale house across the street now had its front light on. A man stood beside the realtor van. His back was turned toward her. He stood tall, an easy six-feet or a couple of inches more. His knee-length black wool coat revealed a trim build, let alone a sharp dresser. His raven-dark hair barely brushed his coat collar. She blinked. Really? She *had* to notice those handsome features. Wait a second. Didn't the boy she'd joined the neighborhood children in mocking also have a similar shade of hair? Back then he wore it a bit long and shaggy. The man her eyes were riveted to had the shorter style she considered attractive on a mature man.

What silliness. She hadn't seen this long-ago classmate in years. Certain he'd go to extremes to avoid her, the chances their paths would never again cross were great in her favor.

She willed away the butterflies flapping in her belly. This was a perfect time for a chocolate intervention. Hmm. Hot chocolate. And she'd also make a mug for Danny. Halfway toward the kitchen, the doorbell rang.

As soon as she opened the door cold air rushed in and the oxygen in her lungs gushed out. Before her stood the realtor,

Helen McCracken, and the last man she expected to see again. Gavin Kinkaid. No doubt.

Possibly her soon-to-be new neighbor, he greeted her with a vanishing smile. His grayish-blue eyes, the color that had always reminded her of a calm lake, darkened to a metallic steel shade often seen in iron fencing. And fences separated two entities...or people. She pressed her trembling hands tight against her legs.

Play it cool. We're both adults now.

His brows arched. "Camille?"

With feet rooted in place as if her fuzzy penguin slippers were cemented to the floor—the ones he now studied with a funny twinkle in his eyes—she couldn't budge an inch. She didn't want to. Her heart pounded. Heat slashed at her cheeks.

She wrapped her arms around her white sweatshirt of a reindeer and its huge red nose. "Hi, Gavin." She cringed at her choppy voice. "I'm surprised you recognize me."

His lips rose in a little, awkward smile. Definitely not a self-satisfied smirk. To be fair, despite the tension between them years ago, she didn't think he was capable of having an attitude. A memory washed over her from when she was sixteen. In full teenage angst she had stormed out of her parents' home and high-tailed it to Kindred Lake, which the town was named after. The two-mile-long body of water separated the downtown section from the residential areas. She wanted to be by herself and ducked behind a tree when she heard someone approaching. That someone was Gavin, and she couldn't stop watching him. No, more like checking him out from head to toe. She'd die if anyone saw her crushing on him...despite the more cool classmates she hung around with ordering her to keep away from him. Her only interaction with Gavin and his family boiled down to hurling insults.

"Camille."

Her name flowing too easily from his lips seized her drifting attention. "Yes?"

"You're someone I could never forget."

$\mathcal{R}$ight out of Gavin's past, this all-grown-up Camille with creamy blondish hair framing a heart-shaped face, the one with a blush caressing her cheeks, was definitely the same Hitchcock girl. If this was any other person her funny house slippers and sweatshirt might have helped to lessen the otherwise awkward situation of inquiring about the neighborhood. Instead, his mouth turned dry. His spine stiffened. The old resentment and hurt surfaced and poked like a pesky bug. Camille, from her well-to-do family, the girl who had acted as if her parents and siblings were better than his own by substantial measures. And now, on the fringe of the holiday season, when he craved the joy of less serious things in life, this was an awful time to be reacquainted with someone he'd hoped to never see again.

He did a double take of the woman before him. Who was he fooling?

The pencil-thin and annoying girl of yesterday had morphed into a stunning, beautiful woman. Her dress-down clothes couldn't disguise those fine looks or curvy figure. He also couldn't deny his reaction. His body heated. His pulse rushed. It was like a buzz sizzled over his skin. Excitement, a feeling he hadn't owned for a while, lifted him up. Ah, get real. This was Camille, and he knew her sorry self too well.

Helen extended a hand toward Camille to shake. "Hello, Mrs. Richardson. It's nice to see you again. You invited me to introduce you to perspective buyers so you could tell them about the neighborhood. If this isn't an inconvenient time, may we visit?"

Gavin tensed. Richardson, huh? So, she was married. Guess those rumors that she'd moved away from Kindred Lake years ago and had remained single were just wild stories. Did she and her husband have a bucketload of kids who also called others bad names? He'd tell Helen he was no longer interested in the house. No way could he live across the street to a woman who still managed to stoke his exasperation. He wouldn't consider it a second longer, and re-buttoned the coat he'd just unfastened.

"Yes, Mrs. McCracken. I remember. Please call me Cami." She smiled at them both. "And you as well, Gavin."

She watched him. For the life of him, he couldn't discern what possibly ran through her mind. Her smile didn't look forced. Her relaxed posture sure didn't signal a self-righteous attitude. Then again, his fiancé fiasco a year ago had taught him the hard way he didn't know much about women.

"Would you like to come in? It's chilly out."

"How nice. And you're to call me Helen." The realtor gestured her client's way. "This is Gavin Kinkaid, but I'm thinking the two of you know each other."

"We're old acquaintances."

The gray-haired woman nodded with enthusiasm. "Wouldn't that be lovely for you two to be neighbors? It's not easy making friends these days." She stepped into the house and looked his way. "Shall we?"

Why not? He was curious to hear what *Cami* had to say after all these years.

Cami dropped her gaze as he walked past her. Actually, more like sank. Right down to those fuzzy, silly slippers that kind of looked adorable on her.

She shut the front door, enveloping them in warmth and a sweet scent. He inhaled deeply.

"Bayberry potpourri. We're trying to get into the holiday mood."

Had her lower lip just quivered? Because of him or the upcoming holidays? Despite their troubled pasts, he didn't like to see her—or anyone—anxious.

This wasn't easy for either one of them. "Great scent."

"Mom," came a shout upstairs.

"My son, Danny." She glanced up. "Come on down, buddy. We have company."

Company. An unexpected word choice from her, but he liked the feel of it. Cozy.

"Mom...your music box. It's all smashed." Danny's gallop downstairs ended a few steps short of his mother. He pulled at the hem of his Spiderman T-shirt. "It's broken. I saw it on your bedroom floor."

Cami patted the boy's arm. "It's okay. Just a box."

"But it was your aunt's. You loved it. You said when you listened to it you wished Dad would dance in circles with you. And now Dad's gone. You'll never dance with him."

"Waltz." Cami closed her eyes for a span of seconds, but it didn't escape Gavin's notice. And all this past-tense talk from Danny about his dad? Either death or divorce. Or possibly no marriage to begin with, though he doubted that was the case here.

"Let's talk more about this later," Cami said. "Say hello to Mr. Kinkaid and Mrs. McCracken, the realtor who is showing Mr. Kinkaid the house for sale. He's thinking about becoming..." She peered directly at him. "I'm sorry. Here I am trying to introduce you and I don't even know if there's a Mrs. Kinkaid and a handful of happy children."

"Just me."

"Oh." The single word puffed from her mouth like a dissipating cloud. She returned her attention to her son. "Well, Mr. Kinkaid might become our new neighbor."

"Call me Gavin, Danny." Fine. He'd give an inch or so. There was no written rule saying he couldn't be civil.

The child paled.

Cami inched closer to her son. "It's fine, honey."

Danny shook his head. "No. It's not. He's the same guy I saw earlier at Friends, like I told you about."

So, Danny was enrolled in the Friends program. The boy

must have seen him this afternoon when he'd stopped by the community center for an interview. He didn't like how his lips were slightly parted and how his brows peaked together. The last thing he wanted was to make a child uncomfortable, especially one who needed an adult Friend the most. And it didn't matter if Danny was Camille...Cami's son.

Worry and sadness laced Cami's green eyes, the very eyes that once vexed him because they'd both repulsed him and attracted him at the same time. The understanding of those cold-warm feelings toward her back then never clicked in his brain. He still didn't know what to make of it. His muddled thoughts weren't important. Her son was enrolled at Friends because he needed an older companion, a man to look up to. Asking the program's director for a different child because he once didn't get along with the his mom wouldn't look good for him, let alone would crush Danny's spirits. On a long-term basis, this might affect his future in child counseling. At the heart of the matter, morally, it would be a lame and immature move. Quite opposite of what he'd been building his adult life around.

He extended his hand for the boy to shake. He aimed for his most affable tone. "It's nice to meet you. I'm looking forward to spending time at Friends."

Danny didn't shake. Gavin slowly withdrew his hand and stuffed it into his coat pocket, keeping a fixed smile.

"Sweetie," Cami said. "Gavin wants to be pals."

The boy focused on the floor. "I'm Danny. Danny Richardson." He then bolted upstairs.

Cami uttered a soft moan. "Danny has struggled through tough times since his dad passed, though he's slowly springing back." She paused, glancing at a green and red fabric Christmas tree on the hall table. "An only child, he's also been lonely, especially this time of year when his classmates are sharing their families' plans for the holidays."

Helen fussed with her scarf. "I'm sorry to hear this. With

Thanksgiving around the corner and Christmas not far off, this can't be an easy time."

"You're right." Cami leveled her gaze directly at him. "Enough with sorrowful thoughts. You have questions about the neighborhood? I'll try to answer them for you."

Had she asked out of obligatory politeness? He caught a look of sincerity in her eyes. Those pretty eyes. It took all of his effort to shift his gaze off of the shade of green that reminded him of a warm spring day.

He could sure use a touch of warmth in his life.

Wait a second. Cami. And this was Cami's house. Any missing comfort wouldn't come from this woman. He took a cursory look, determined to find proof that she was the same disagreeable Camille he'd been too familiar with.

Instead, he was surrounded by homey touches. Earthy colors of red, brown, and yellow enhanced the living room. Two framed antique mottos hung over a table with a vase full of dried flowers. One had *In God We Trust* stitched in purple embroidery. The other, in gold lettering, read *Love and Respect*. Photos lined the shelves of a bookcase filled with paperbacks.

He rubbed the back of his neck. Outwardly, Cami had changed into a beauty. Maybe, she'd changed within as well. He mentally shook his head. Nope. He wasn't going to go there. He'd had it with chameleon women who changed their ways to suit their own desires. There would be no return to see what other stunts she could pull. But, there was no reason why he couldn't act civil to her or to her son.

"You've made a pleasant home here, Cami."

"Thanks. Nice neighbors can help with a sense of coziness."

Back to business. Good. He refocused on the reason behind his visit.

"Is the neighborhood on the quiet side?"

"Quiet is its best feature. Since this road T's into Lake Road, there's not much thru traffic. We're fortunate to live by Kindred

Lake without crazy property taxes. And it's such a beautiful lake... Todd and I took so many walks..." She hugged her middle. "I still get choked up with memories."

His own gut squeezed with empathy. "I can understand."

She ran a hand through her hair. "The young kids play in each other's backyards and the teens manage to keep to themselves by hanging out at the town park along the lake, which keeps them out of trouble. Everyone is friendly but manages to keep their noses out of anyone's business." She pressed her left hand against her mouth. "Sorry," she said around her fingers. "That was bold."

He couldn't help notice the lack of a wedding band, but returned his attention to the topic. "I didn't take it personally."

Helen shifted her purse to the other hand and back again. "The house across the street is perfect for a single man."

Did the older woman serve as the neighborhood's part-time matchmaker? Not that he wanted to explore that route.

"Let me check my calendar." Helen pulled out her cell phone. "The people I have booked tomorrow morning to see the house are desperate for a place to live due to a relocation situation—a circumstance happening more and more these days. The owners are quite eager to move. They're willing to do what they can to expedite the sale."

What a fine mess he'd waddled into. He longed for a place of his own. And ever since he'd left this town, he'd miss the two-mile narrow lake that had supplied him with the few pleasant childhood memories he'd enjoyed. The house itself was a perfect fit for him. Well kept, unlike his childhood home. The place was small, yet had a smart floor-layout making the house feel roomy. He could easily convert the second bedroom into the office he'd dreamed about. There was a room off the living room where he could settle down with his studies...a den. After a workshop, a den was every man's desire.

Ah, yes. His child counselor studies. Quiet. The exact reason he stood before his childhood adversary to ironically inquire about the tranquility of the neighborhood. In his wildest dreams he'd never thought twice about running into Cami, and what she represented, let alone becoming neighbors. If he were to purchase the house, he'd bump into her often. Most likely, daily, just in passing. Could he put aside their differences?

At this stage of his life, he wanted a fresh start and didn't want more delays. He faced Helen. "I'll take the house."

The woman's eyes sparkled. "You'll enjoy your new home immensely. Everyone will welcome you into the neighborhood."

He pulled at his chin while he studied Cami. "I'm up for friendly neighbors."

After they exchanged goodnights, he headed to his car. He slid behind the wheel. About to start the engine, he squeezed the ignition key so tight in his palm that he flinched.

He was back in town on the hope he'd mend the relationship with his father. Years ago, he'd made a vow to Pop to keep away from Cami and anyone else that had singled out his family for living differently than their more influential upper-class ways. As Cami's new neighbor, this reconciliation with Pop wasn't going to be easy. If it happened at all.

He glanced upward. "Okay, God. What exactly do you have up Your sleeve by reuniting me with Cami?"

2

*C*ami's new neighbor moved into his house the first week of December. If anyone had hinted months ago that it would be Gavin Kinkaid she'd surely have raided the chocolate aisle in the market and stocked up months of supplies. The closing happened fast, even for this small town. That he bought the house across from her in the first place was amazing.

Ever since that November evening when she saw the one person from her past she never banked becoming neighbors with, her concentration was pretty well shot. Dressed handsomely in his dark dress coat that highlighted his mesmerizing eyes, he first appeared to be a woman's gift-wrapped fantasy come true. But, he wasn't her dream. It was more like she was his nightmare. He must despise her. What happened in the past surely shaped who he was today. And marked her in his mind as the forever bad person.

She needed to watch her step. If word were to spread about the way she'd once treated him, her reputation as a caring woman in charge of children would suffer. A big risk to her career. Against her pleading, Todd had canceled his life insurance policy. Her income meant feast or famine for Danny and her.

"Mom," Danny shouted from upstairs.

In the bright yellow and green kitchen, Cami finished wrapping her son's PBJ sandwich for school and placed it into his favorite action-figure hero lunch box. She then started upstairs only to find Danny at the top of the landing. He leaned on his elbows propped on his knees. Her serious thinker zinged her mom heart.

"What's up, Snickers bar?"

Danny giggled. "I can't find my sneakers."

"They're in your gym bag. Wear your boots since it might snow and change at school."

His eyes brightened. "You mean, I'll get out of school early?"

"Don't know, bud. Right now it's decent weather. Let's go before you miss the bus." Although Little Bears operated from seven in the morning to six in the evening, Cami was staffed properly to cover different shifts. Three days a week she worked the later time period. It allowed for more time with Danny, like breakfast and taking him to the bus. Afterwards he attended the Friend program. The other two days she relied on a sitter to get Danny off to school and then she herself would be home for her little sunshine.

Danny padded his way down the steps. Almost out of time, she helped him into both his boots and coat. She also managed to grab their lunches. Finally, they were outdoors, breathing in the fresh cool December air. They crossed the street.

"Look, Mom." Danny stopped before their new neighbor's house. "Gavin decorated his house with Christmas lights. They look awesome. Can we put up ours?"

"We're not competing."

"I know. I just like them. Christmas lights make everything sparkly and special."

Cami looked at their house and flinched. She could think of

many other ways of experiencing fun other than balancing the strings of outdoor lights on a ladder. As independent as she was, for a moment she wished she had Todd back...a man to help her, love her. Nonsense. Todd always made an unpleasant fuss. She'd hang the lights herself.

"How about today when I get home from work?"

When no response came, she turned around and discovered it difficult to coordinate breathing and thinking.

"Hi, neighbors," Gavin called as he—and the most adorable puppy she'd ever seen—strode down the sidewalk toward them.

"Mom, look." Danny pointed to the puppy whose tail wagged like life was one big summer picnic. Mere seconds later Danny hunched his shoulders. "Let's go to the bus stop before he gets here."

Was Danny holding tight onto resentment against Gavin taking his former Friend's place? Cami placed her mitten-covered hand on Danny's shoulder, determined to set a positive example unlike the one her own parents had taught regarding friendliness to others. She smiled at Gavin who now stood before them. The response had come easier and more satisfying than she'd anticipated as if greeting him was an everyday, natural experience.

"Hello, there." She slipped off her mittens and stooped to pet the puppy. "Aren't you the cutest thing?"

Gavin scooped up the wiggling puppy and tucked it under his arm. "This little guy is Happy. We just adopted each other last week."

She ignored Danny's tug on her coat. "Oooh, perfect name. Is he ever happy."

"He's been one little energetic fur ball of joy since I brought him home, brightening my life as well."

His life needed a bit of sparkle? She blinked, redirecting her thoughts back to the puppy. "Is he a yellow lab?"

"He is. With my studies, I didn't think a pup would be a wise choice for my busy lifestyle, but when a friend introduced us there was no way I could say no to this little guy. Talk about love at first sight."

Love? Stick to safer topics, she reminded herself. "Your studies?"

Danny pointed to the corner. "Come on, Mom. I don't want to miss the bus."

The three of them stood facing each other, with Happy still squirming in Gavin's arms. The lack of Danny's invitation to accompany them was as palpable as the oncoming change of weather. Gavin's eyes didn't conceal emotion well, past or present, and darkened with disappointment. Her heart sagged a little for him.

"It's okay," he said.

Could it be okay, given their sad past?

He jutted his chin at Danny. "What grade are you in, chief?"

Danny squared his shoulders back. "Chief? No one has ever called me chief before."

"Yep. Chief. You're a top guy." Gavin extended his palm for a high five.

"Wow," Danny said. He slapped Gavin's waiting palm. Then, as if he'd pondered on the nickname's significance, he shrugged. "Ah, it's just a name. I'm in third grade. I'm in Mrs...." His mouth dropped open.

Cami rubbed at her own smarting jaw. "He's in Mrs. Kinkaid's class." She wiggled her finger between Gavin and an imaginary person beside him. "Am I thinking she's your..."

He grinned. Her heart tugged a funny wee bit.

"Yep, she's my mother. Mom began teaching after you and I entered junior high."

"She can't be your mother," Danny stated. "She's totally cool. I like her. And my mom's a teacher too."

The loud hiss of the school bus coming to a stop announced the time and axed the conversation between the three of them.

Cami planted a kiss on her son's forehead. "You have a good day at school."

Danny smiled then shot Gavin a narrow-eyed look. "Be careful, Mom." He ran to the corner where the bus waited with its door open.

"Danny?" What was that about? She watched him climb the steps into the bus. Only after the vehicle swept him away did she face Gavin.

He beat her to words. "Your little guy is certainly looking out for you."

"I'm sorry." She slipped her mittens back on. "I'm not sure of what's going through Danny's mind lately. I doubt he's aware of his words at times."

"I understand. Sounds like a lot of emotions are riding his shoulders."

"Losing his dad has been rough. You're right about the emotions." She sighed. "A lot of ups and down. And I confess, me too."

He grasped her upper arm. A gentle touch. A caring touch. Couldn't be. A tingle tickled its way to her shoulder.

"I imagine it's difficult for both of you."

Her eyes were level with his chest and the puppy. Cute and cuddly. Both of them.

"I should go." She couldn't place one foot in front of another to get away from Gavin. Nor, did she want to.

The puppy wiggled and pawed at the momentary edge creeping between them like a crack of cold wind.

She noticed a pair of gloves sticking out from Gavin's jacket pocket. She reached for the puppy. "Here, let me take this bundle of joy for a couple of minutes. Your hands must be cold."

"Thanks." He rubbed his bare hands then stuffed them into his gloves. "What do you teach and where?"

"I taught kindergarten for a couple of years before Danny was born. I've since become a director of a preschool."

"The Little Bears on North Boulevard?"

"Yes." She trembled. She couldn't tell if her reaction stemmed from the surprise over the ease of conversing, or his genuine interest in knowing more about her.

"Impressive."

"Yeah, well, I know I'm young..." She grinned. "Why am I telling you this? Of course you know. We're the same age."

"I'm sure you worked hard to get where you are." He leaned back and smiled. "And I'm sure that's an understatement."

"Of the year." She shook again.

"You're cold," he said before she could reply. "Let me walk you back home."

She scratched under the puppy's chin. "Only if I get to hold Happy. His warmth is better than the thickest of woolen blankets. Besides, he's too adorable to put down."

"I'm teaching him everything vital in life, including how to charm the neighbors."

She pulled the puppy tighter against her and stroked between his ears. Unsure of what to reply, she didn't dare look up at Gavin.

Once across the street, he slid his gloves off and reached to pet the dog and brushed against her hand. Her gaze roamed from their hands up his arm and into his grayish blue eyes.

"Don't be nervous, Cami. Happy will keep me in line. Bonus."

She chuckled. "I like your sense of humor. So, I'll wave a hi-neighbor when we meet at our mailboxes or grab the newspaper from its box?"

"I wouldn't want it any other way." Happy yipped and kicked his tiny legs. "Looks like he wants his papa." Gavin took the struggling puppy from her. "Is it just you and your son? I mean, is there a boyfriend? Don't mean to be nosy, but knowing might help me be a better Friend to Danny."

"My husband passed away three years ago. Danny was five at the time." She petted Happy between his ears. The puppy barked in gratitude. "No dates. Between my son and work, I'm kept plenty busy." And that was just fine with her. One fragmented relationship in a lifetime was all she could handle. Hot tears stung her eyes. She turned away.

Her foot caught on a patch of ice and she began to slip.

He caught her by the elbow. He pulled her closer, with the wiggly puppy pressed between them. "I got you. You're okay."

Confident words. Reassuring words.

Happy became tangled on his leash. Gavin laughed and lifted the pup into the air. "What a mess you've gotten yourself into." He proceeded to gently and easily separate dog and leash.

"You're really patient with him." She decided not to hold back the other thoughts begging to float free from her mouth. "How about you? Were you married? Have children?"

"Never been married. No kids." He set the puppy on the ground. "After high school I joined the Air Force."

"Oh, wow. Are you becoming a commercial pilot? Is that what you're studying?"

"Nah. You couldn't keep me away from getting the bad guys, and anything with big wings and engines." A boyish grin crossed his face. "But I'm a small-town guy. Just itching to settle down and grow roots. I care about people. Specifically children. Now that I'm out of the Air Force I'm studying child counseling."

"Helping others..."

He looked into her eyes. "A lot of folks have it rough these days. I'm happy when others are happy."

She glanced at her watch. "I have to grab my briefcase and get to work."

"I'll see you around."

"Guess so."

She petted the puppy one last time and started toward her front door.

"Hey, Cami," he called.

She paused.

"Have a good day, neighbor."

"Yeah, you too."

She hurried indoors for her briefcase and purse. She was going to have to be careful. She was finished hurting others. First Gavin. Then her husband. Never, ever her son.

*C*ami swung into Little Bears' parking lot, aware of the odd flutter weaving between her ribs while she mused over Gavin. In the Air Force, huh? He liked kids and animals. And he was nice to her, not showing the agitation a former foe might emanate. He'd physically reached out to her, but more to keep her from falling on the ice, right? And this neighbor thing he'd mentioned? Surely that was his way of reminding her that she lived on her side of the road and he on the other. And, it was best to respect each other's personal space.

Enough thinking. She slipped into supervisor mode and started the day's work.

The approaching storm and the various winter illnesses circulating cut attendance in half. The next hour flew by, full of activity. When the snow-ice mixture began to fall and the public schools were dismissed at noon, the phone-tree activated. Parents arrived quickly to whisk their young ones home. By the time the last child breezed out the door it was already two in the afternoon. Finally, the staff could leave.

The bad road conditions made for slow driving. An early school closing meant no Friends meeting. Although Danny had his own key to get into the house during a rare early dismissal, Cami hated the idea he would be home alone. It was bad enough she suffered from the holiday blues, but she didn't want her son by himself and growing lonely.

When she turned the engine off in her driveway, she listened to the calming silence that only falling snow could bring. They were safe at home, unharmed by the storm.

Her inner peace lasted but ten seconds when she pushed open her front door.

No lights were on. "Danny?"

No reply. Or footsteps. Or giggles from a hiding Danny waiting to surprise her. She began to look for a note he might have left.

The phone rang. It better be Danny.

"Mom. It's me."

"Hi, my sweets," she said, her breath falling hard into the phone. "Where are you?"

"At Gavin's. Come on over. He baked cookies for us."

Cookies? "But—"

"See ya soon." He hung up.

Danny greeted her at Gavin's door before she rang the door-bell. Chocolate adorned his lips in a lopsided mustache.

"Hi, Mom. What took you so long?"

He snatched her hand and began to tug her indoors. She managed to push the door shut with a hip and to stomp the snow from her boots onto the doormat.

"Come on, Gavin baked the greatest cookies ever." He led her through the living room. Although they moved quickly she glimpsed a few framed photographs on the shelf over his stereo. One large photo of three men and one woman in military uniforms hung over his sofa. A Bible faced open on the coffee table. People and faith. Evidently, both mattered highly to him.

Funny how the *nice* older couple who used to live here had never invited them into their house over the years. Now, she and Danny were guests. Wait a second. Danny, she reminded herself. Gavin probably asked Danny in when he saw her son arrive home and her car was gone. Simple. Neighborly. He couldn't care less about her.

But didn't Danny say distinctly that Gavin had baked cookies for both of them, not just Danny?

She sighed when her son yanked her hand. "Easy. You don't have to pull so hard."

"Yeah, I do. You're walking slow, like you don't want to see Gavin."

Her face heated. The man in question probably stood around the corner in ear's reach.

Danny pulled her into a small but cozy off-white kitchen with salmon trim. From under the table, Happy yipped. Gavin, wearing snug jeans, a wintergreen pullover sweater, and no shoes, only thick woolen gray socks wrapped around large feet, leaned over the open oven door and removed a tray of cookies. Her heart jumped a funny little jig.

The sugary aroma of chocolate and buttery hot dough wafted past her and she hoped her stomach wouldn't growl in betrayal. How did Gavin know her two weaknesses in life: chocolate cookies and men who could bake them?

"They're chocolate chunk and pecan cookies." Gavin said. "Have a seat. There's fresh coffee brewing and I'm dishing out a second round of cookies. Like chocolate?"

She swallowed twice. "Oh, yeah. We bonded years ago."

Danny climbed onto a chair. "Like this kind of surprise, Mom?"

"Now that I know you're safe, sure. This is a nice surprise."

Gavin set the red Santa-shaped dish, stacked full of delectable cookies, center on the table. "I know it's early to break out the holiday dishes, but with the first major snow coming down I figured why not." He gestured toward the platter heaped with the sweet treats.

She hesitated. "We should go. You've had enough interruptions to the peace and quiet you'd hoped for when purchasing this house."

He lifted a brow. "You're no intrusion."

"I don't want to go, Mom," Danny said in full whine.

Happy barked, as if to side with his new young pal.

"I saw Danny walking toward the house when he got off the school bus earlier. Since you weren't home I invited him in, thinking you wouldn't mind. I've enjoyed his company. I'll like it too if you visit with me for a while."

Danny grabbed a cookie. "Yeah, Mom. I've had fun with Gavin and Happy."

Cami's fisted breathing eased. With big smiles and wide eyes, the two guys certainly looked as if they'd enjoyed each other's companionship, the earlier strife between them while Danny waited for the school bus gone. "All right. Thanks, Gavin." She was surprised how effortlessly his name rolled from her mouth, and how fast she shimmied out of her jacket.

"That's what neighbors are about. Helping each other. Short and simple."

She wouldn't exactly think of simple as the best way to describe him, their close proximity as neighbors, or her growing curiosity about him.

"I appreciate it, though please don't feel obligated each time there's a school closing. I probably should arrange for the bus to drop Danny at Little Bears."

"No, Mom." Danny said. "I'm too old to hang out with little kids."

Gavin pushed the cookie platter toward her. "The chief has a point."

Her son giggled—probably at the mention of his new nickname.

Gavin's smile further won her over. Oh, those nice even teeth of his.

"Have a cookie, Cami."

Cami. He had made her name sound like a symphony. She accepted the chocolate treat without delay.

"It's been a while since I've baked and fussed over someone."

She knew that sense of emptiness intimately. She wouldn't wish it on anyone.

She bit into the cookie. A satisfied moan escaped her mouth. Forget diets. She selected two more, big ones studded with candy chunks, and placed them on a napkin. She licked melting chocolate from her thumb. "These are the yummiest I've ever tasted."

Gavin eyed Danny conspiratorially. "Well, chief, I guess my cookies rate."

Cami leaned back to enjoy this new connection between man and boy. Her shoulders and back muscles uncoiled. Gavin did have a gentle way with children.

And he had a nice way with her.

He reached for another cookie. "Thanks. It's an old recipe handed down through the generations of bakers in my family. When I was younger, I'd come home from school and my mom or sisters would always have a snack baking. Pies, breads, cookies. Name it. It would be either rising, expanding, or oozing sweetness in that old oven of ours."

Cami used to envision the kind of life the Kinkaid family lived within the desperately-in-need-of-paint house. Somehow, the family hearth and good food with the memories that often came attached with them weren't part of what she'd imagined. His past sorely contrasted to her memories of her own family's elegant Victorian home in fine condition, both inside and out. The house was well built and sizable, regal if anything, but she couldn't recall the scent of baked goods welcoming her home from school. Nor could she remember being greeted, period.

She clasped her hands around the mug of coffee Gavin had handed her. The smell of hazelnut tickled her nose. Her favorite. She took a sip and caught him watching.

"Decaffeinated. Tossing and turning all night isn't fun."

"Most considerate. Again." She took another sip. Her gaze locked with his welcoming eyes. "Sounds like a bunch of nice memories you have of a close family."

"We are close...were close. I've been out of touch lately. Another reason why I'm glad I moved back to town. Guess you can say I'm a family kind-of-guy. I'm hoping to shorten the gap between all of us. Mainly the trouble is between Pop and me."

"My family keeps its distance, too." She set her eyes on Danny who sat on the floor playing with the puppy. "My parents didn't approve of Todd," she said softly.

"Or you marrying him?"

She nodded. "They didn't approve of anything I chose to do or..." She swallowed hard. "Or anyone I loved." She waited to see if he'd toss out a caustic barb, but none came. "Makes me love my son more," she said louder to reach Danny's ears.

"Aw, Mom."

She smiled at her son. "Want to go out and play in the snow before dinnertime? That is, if we both have room for dinner after nibbling on this feast."

Danny jumped to his feet, grabbed a handful of cookies and his coat, and darted toward the door. Happy followed, his tail wagging.

"I should be on my way too. The public schools might be canceled tomorrow, but daycare will be open."

"Relax. Stay another moment or two." He topped off her mug with more coffee.

She didn't have time to rest. Yet she couldn't resist his offer. "For a short while. I have tons of paperwork to sort through after dinner, and a promise to keep that I'd made to Danny. I'm glad he's not fussy when it comes to supper, though he probably won't want a full size meal after indulging in these heavenly cookies." She reached for another. "I hope you don't mind."

A grin lit his face; his eyes twinkled. "Help yourself."

"Looks like it's canned soup tonight."

He gave a thumbs up. "Soup's my kind of dinner on a cold winter night." He ran a fingertip around the rim of his mug. "Danny's a great kid. I enjoyed our time together this afternoon. Sure hope it will work out at Friends for the two of us."

"You two have grown closer."

He winked. "Sweets can soothe the masses."

"It certainly worked with my son."

The phone rang. He waved it off. "The answering machine will get it."

About to tease him over using an outdated machine rather than voicemail, she stopped short at his frown. The speaker used a gruff tone and sounded vaguely familiar.

"Gavin," an older man's voice broadcasted. "It's me. Pick up."

"My pop," Gavin mouthed.

She motioned that she could leave. He signaled for her to stay.

"Listen, son," his pop continued. "I know it's been a while since we've last spoken. I have lots to talk about with you."

Gavin leaned back and crossed his arms. Cami remembered he'd said he and his dad were at odds with each other.

"Your mom's informed me who you're living next door to. I don't like it one bit. What's gotten into your foolish brain?"

Gavin's forehead furrowed. Cami couldn't tell if the twinge of red swiping his cheeks was anger or shame over his dad.

"Pay attention to what I'm saying. Tell your neighbor to keep her distance from you."

Gavin sprang to his feet. "Enough." In a couple of strides he switched off the recording device. He pivoted away. The corner of the machine caught in the cuff of his sweater. It thudded to the floor, letting loose a few mechanical rings.

Cami stood, hugging her middle. "Looks like the old resentment about me has never quite faded. I can't blame your dad." She stared at the damaged answering machine. "And I can't blame you either, Gavin, for the awkward vibes between us." She grabbed her jacket from the back of the chair. "I shouldn't try to pretend I wasn't horrible to you."

"Hold on," he called.

Danny skidded into the kitchen. Happy trotted behind, playfully snapping at his boots.

"Happy doesn't like the snow. He won't stay out." Danny's eyes widened at the machine on the floor. "Whoa. What happened?" Cami placed a hand on Danny's shoulder and started to guide him toward the door where he probably left his coat. She stopped. She was assuming a lot. Like she knew the location of her son's coat. Like she had the right to walk about Gavin...her neighbor's house, unescorted, as if it were her place. Like old grudges could be forgotten about easily. Willingly.

Danny sidestepped away. He searched first her eyes then Gavin's, who had followed right behind them. "Did you two fight?"

"No...we didn't." That was the big thing. They hadn't argued. They'd enjoyed each other's company. It was like their past troubles had never occurred and they were first getting to know each other. And it had felt so nice.

"Danny," Gavin said. "We were talking and having fun when the phone rang. When I went to turn off the answering machine it caught on my sweater and landed on the floor."

Danny studied them. "Good. I don't want you to fight."

"Me neither," Cami and Gavin said in unison.

They looked at each other and grinned.

Cami spotted Danny's coat slung over the couch's arm. "It's late. Time to go home, hon. Get into your coat."

"Why? We just live across the street."

She glanced at Gavin. Yes, they did live across the street from each other. There was no escaping the truth. It was time for their families to accept the situation.

While respect for others was disregarded when she was a child, she'd vowed to herself when she learned she was pregnant with Danny that she would instill good values in her son. "Thank Gavin for the nice time you had this afternoon, and for inviting you into his home after school."

Danny stepped up to Gavin. "Thanks. I had a great time here with you and Happy."

"I did too. We're neighbors and friends."

"See, Mom. There's nothing to worry about."

Cami thanked Gavin and wished him a goodnight. It was only when she opened the door and faced the dark and cold of a winter night did she question the no-worry part.

3

*C*ami yielded to Danny's request to stay outdoors while she finished her paperwork. He'd been determined to build a snowman. She doubted his luck with only three inches of snow, thankfully far less than originally forecasted. Though, she wasn't about to discourage him. Then it would be suppertime, followed by stringing the outdoor Christmas lights, then off to bed. By then, they'd exhaust the ample supply of cookie-sugar energy scored at Gavin's.

Gavin.

A neighbor whose dad wasn't thrilled she lived directly opposite from his son.

As she opened the can of tomato soup for Danny—she had zilch appetite—she glanced out the kitchen window wondering how to dodge further questions from Danny regarding Gavin. Foolishness pretty much summarized her stray thoughts over whether they could start anew. With his family perpetuating tension, as expressed too clearly in his father's phone call, peace between them didn't stand a chance. Then again, the senior Kinkaid was entitled to his opinions.

She cringed.

Would forgiveness ever factor into this equation? At this point, she doubted the possibility. Then again, Gavin might not side with his dad. This was confusing and draining. No wonder her energy level had suddenly plunged like a rock falling down a cliff, bumping against all the jagged edges along its path.

Her hand slipped. A finger scraped the can's cut top.

Ouch.

She grabbed a paper towel and pressed it against her bleeding finger. She'd live. But all she wanted was to experience a little sliver of happiness, if not for her, for Danny. If she remained stuck, twisted in these tangled emotions over a man she had no right to think twice about, only more trouble would brew. And she'd had it with trouble.

She also didn't want to see Gavin burdened. He didn't deserve it. No one deserved emotional anguish.

The side door banged open. "Mom?"

She patted her pounding heart. "Hungry?"

"Not yet." Danny stepped closer. He pointed to her finger with the towel wrapped tight around it. "Are you hurt?"

"Just a little nick from opening the can. I'm fine."

"Good. Let's string the lights."

So much for sympathy.

"It's getting late, buddy."

"But you said it's supposed to be real cold tomorrow. It's not bad right now. Can we, Mom? Please."

She zeroed in on her son's happiness. "Let's do it."

Her beautiful boy whooped then grew serious. "You know, you're a pretty cool mom."

She mussed his static-filled hair. "Thanks, sweetheart."

"Gavin thinks so too."

"How would he know?"

"'Cause I told him about the neat things you do for me."

She pulled Danny to her side. "What a nice thing to say."

"Gavin said it first. He said he could see love in your eyes for me, Mom. And he says 'cause Dad's gone you have to do a lot for me. He says you do stuff for me without umbles."

Umbles? "Do you mean grumbles?"

"Yep. He said it's obvious."

Warmth chased away the chill she couldn't shake since leaving Gavin's house earlier that evening. "Thanks for sharing. I love you, my little man."

He thumbed his chest. "Me? But Gavin said those things. I just agreed with him."

"Ready for stringing those holiday lights?"

His forehead crinkled with the change of subject. "Uh...yeah."

"I'll grab my coat and boots."

*N*o problems arose from buttoning up again for the cold, or from lugging the box of lights from the basement. Moving the ladder from its tight spot in the garage didn't prove to be difficult, either. Cami counted on the front post light at the foot of the drive to cast sufficient illumination to accomplish the task. Easy-peasy. She could only hope.

"Let's begin, Danny." Together, they leaned the ladder against the fir tree in the front yard. With the roll of lights wrapped around her shoulder, she started to climb. "It's a good thing I don't fear heights." Somehow, her tone didn't sound convincing to her own ears.

"Can you reach where Dad marked the X? It looks great there."

She agreed and climbed another rung. "I see the spot, but I can't reach it."

"Do you have a stick to push up the lights?"

"You're a clever thinker. I'll grab the garden rake from the garage."

When she emerged from the garage minutes later with rake in hand, her mouth dropped open. The tree shined brightly with its lights neatly wrapped around, twinkling flashes of gold and silver. Side by side, Gavin and Danny stood in silent admiration of its beauty.

She clomped through the snow toward her neighbor and beaming son. Shivers poked down her spine. "Danny?"

"It's not want you're thinking, Mom. I didn't go anywhere. Gavin came to help us."

She nodded. Danny never fibbed.

Danny swooshed the snow side to side with the toe of his boot. "He watched us out his window. Like when we watched him the day he looked at his house with the realtor lady."

A chuckle escaped Gavin's lips.

Oh oh. She covered her face. Was it possible to blush in freezing temperatures? Curiosity took over. She peeked to see a smile lifting Gavin's lips...his handsome, manly lips. The tight knot wedged deep within her ever since she arrived home from his place loosened. A cackle escaped from her mouth. She covered her lips, but couldn't stop. Soon, all three were laughing. Together. It felt good. So very good.

When she caught her breath she faced Gavin. "I can assure you I'm no damsel in distress."

His dazzling eyes met her gaze. "I would never link you to the DDU."

"Pardon?"

"The distressed damsel union."

"Cute." She smiled. It was as if a toasty fireplace was lit in the cold outdoors just for the three of them. "The tree looks nice."

A sneaky grin played with his mouth. "Like it, huh?"

"Yes. It looks amazing. Thanks."

"Danny says you also decorate the garage." He glanced over his shoulder at the exterior building. "Want me to help?"

"Cool," Danny answered before Cami could say otherwise.

She couldn't get out of this deepening situation between the three of them. That was okay. She didn't want to. "Let's get a move on it then before the temp drops more." She glanced at this man from her past and thought twice about the temperature. It wasn't cold out, after all.

4

*L*ast night's attempt at decent sleeping was a joke. At four in the morning, with images of Cami re-playing in Gavin's brain, he flung the warm blankets off. On the edge of the bed, he scrubbed his hands over the morning stubble on his cheeks, the burn spreading from his fingers up his forearms. The thing was, he'd enjoyed every second he'd spent with Cami yesterday evening when he helped decorate her place with the Christmas lights. When they called it quits and parted with goodnights, he uneasily retreated indoors. Now, although Happy tried his best to cheer him with puppy antics, loneliness hit hard like a punch to the gut.

"Want to help unpack some boxes?"

His furry companion yipped.

"Let's go, partner."

They padded into the future den where he rolled his eyes at the clutter. Yep, no one would doubt a bachelor lived here, all right. How had he accumulated so much stuff in such a short time? He unpeeled masking tape from carton after carton, shoveling out crumpled newspaper and bubble wrap and playfully tossing it on top of Happy. He wasn't sure who had the most fun. At daybreak, he eased into his much beloved cozy recliner. A coffee carafe sat shotgun beside him on an end table. Happy snoozed, draped across his brown corduroy slippers.

Slippers. Cami's penguin slippers. Cami. She'd look stunning in whatever she wore. A casual work outfit. Weekend jeans and a hoodie. A slinky black evening dress...with black heels for dancing.

He rubbed his eyes at his over-zealous imagination and grunted. With one shove, he jumped from the chair. The puppy rolled off his feet, his mouth exploded in a yawn.

"Sorry, boy." He scratched Happy's chin. The pup rewarded him with a playful bark. "I have a plan of action forming fast and furious. Got to get a move on it."

Never daunted by the cold, Gavin stuffed his feet into his insulated boots, bundled into his jacket, and threw open the front door. A strong blast of wind whipped by, carrying sounds of a faulty car engine starting then stalling. Across the road at Cami's the hood of her car was open. He hurried over.

Bent over the car, Cami groaned.

Unable to move his gaze away from her perfect curves, he paused.

"Once more, Danny."

Her son, in the driver's seat, turned and caught site of Gavin. They exchanged waves.

Danny slid out from the car. "Mom, guess who's here?"

"I can't understand you with this wind," she shouted. "Try cranking it again."

"I can help," Gavin offered.

Cami snapped upright, her hand covering her heart.

"Didn't mean to scare you. Does the engine turn over?"

"Yes, but it doesn't want to stay engaged. I tried feathering it then put it into gear and the stupid beast died on me."

"Have recent work done on the car?"

"Just had a new computer installed. It better be good for the price I paid."

"I bet I know the problem. Do you have tools? Wrenches?"

"In the trunk."

She stared at him. For a second he fantasized that her intense scrutiny meant she liked what she saw, but he couldn't fool himself. It probably was more of a case of her wondering what was behind his motive to help, or whether he was even capable of car repair.

Nope. This old way of thinking wasn't going to benefit either of them.

The cold temperature snaked around his neck. "Cami?" he gently prodded.

A deep flush brushed her cheeks a rosy shade. He'd love to tease her, but held back.

She plodded through the snow and withdrew a slim toolbox from the trunk. "Don't know where my mind is at times. It's probably frozen." She fetched her keys from her coat pocket. "Danny, go wait indoors."

They both watched him barrel toward the house.

Gavin tightened the computer ground. "I'm working on a hunch, but give it another try."

She slid into the driver's seat, keeping the window rolled down. The engine kicked over and this time remained running. She cheered in relief.

"I had the same problem once. My pop, a whiz auto mechanic, taught me the trick of trouble-shooting, at least when it comes to cars." He leaned against the open driver's window. "Trouble-shooting life is a whole different story."

"Oh, how I know that aggravation too." She sighed. "With everything going wrong, I wonder what the rest of the day will be like."

He shook his head, clearing his mind of desires he shouldn't dream about. "That bad?"

She stepped out of the car. "I'm late for work, Danny's school is closed, and his babysitter's husband's sick, plus *her* car won't start. I offered to pick her up, but then my car wouldn't start. Until you..."

Her words slid somewhere into her scarf. Her forehead knotted. He wanted to tuck her into his arms and keep her there.

"You bailed me out again, Gavin. Thank you."

"You're welcome, but I haven't performed a miracle."

She stamped snow from her boots. "You did. You helped me."

"And that ranks up there?"

"I'm not accustomed to help. I wouldn't have expected any from..." She whipped her hand over her mouth.

"From me?" Her sparkling eyes drew him with magnetic force. "Right before coming over here I realized the need to leave the past behind once and for all. I think God's gracing me with making us neighbors. Care to join me in ditching what happened in our yesterdays?"

Cami glanced over at Danny who shuffled his way toward them in baby-sized steps. "I don't think I can."

Chills pricked his arms. So, she couldn't shove aside the past. Was it a case of not wanting to let go and move on? Something more? More like she plain didn't like him, at all? Yet, he knew better than to be self-centered, to think the world wrapped around him.

Anguish clouded her eyes.

He swallowed hard, inching closer to her. "When I'm stuck, I pray, believing with all my heart that God hears me and wants to help."

"Good advice, if you believe God wants to intervene." She glanced again at her son. "Will you listen to whiny me? Sorry. Thanks for your help. I better get Danny's sitter."

She needed comforting.

He wanted to comfort her.

He trailed his fingers slowly to her shoulder. Layers of

clothing separated his fingertips from her bare arm, but some kind of wild spark jumped between them. Did she feel it too? He murmured her name. Their gazes locked.

"If it's any comfort, Cami, know I'll be praying for you today. I believe God will help you. He wants to help."

"Me?"

He nodded. "He loves each one of us."

"Mom," Danny said. "Work phoned. I said you'd call back."

"Probably someone calling out sick." She licked her lips. "I guess this God thing is another difference between us."

"Then, I'll pray daily for you."

"You'd do that for me?"

"Definitely."

"Because you don't want a gap between us?"

He paused, aware of his genuine answer. "Well, honestly, yes." He didn't avert his gaze from hers. "But also, it's because God wants to love you as His daughter."

She smiled a little. "Maybe God will get tired of hearing my name and give me a break. For now, I better phone into work." With the car running, she hurried indoors.

The belief of God looking after Cami flooded Gavin with renewed peace. He watched her, ignoring the worsening wind. She had a cute trot, his snow bunny. His snow bunny? *His?* Where did that come from? He'd mentioned closing the space between them, as in friendship, as in getting along. Nothing else. Right?

❋

*I*n her usually chilly office, Cami sat behind her desk, enjoying unexpected warmth spreading throughout her insides. Wow. Gavin had offered to pray for her. She couldn't remember anyone offering to do so, or for that matter, thinking twice about her, except for her Auntie Fran. Although her family might have attended church every Sunday while she was growing up, and observed the holidays with the customary traditions, she couldn't remember prayers or praises to God shared between her parents or sisters. At times, she'd wondered if it was more like keeping up a social reputation as a *good family*. Definitely not a demonstration of faith. Now an adult, she wanted to believe in God. Yet, doubt over her worth in His eyes plagued her heart. God couldn't love her. Not when Todd died the way he did. Not when she was behind the misery of others in those dark childhood years of hers.

The phone rang. "Little Bears. Camille Richardson speaking. May I help you?" She listened to yet another faculty member call out due to the flu bug circulating, and silently groaned. "I understand, Lisa. Rest and get better soon."

The phone buzzed again. She cast it a wary look as she picked up the receiver. About to give her standard greeting, Danny's sitter blurted both Danny and she had fevers. Plus, she was walking home before she couldn't, and not to worry because she'd called Gavin and he was watching Danny.

Of course she'd worry about her son, as well as be concerned for the young sitter, but first she'd have to rush around and get things done so she could get home. And then there was Gavin. She owed him an apology for the way the sitter drafted him into taking her place. He'd moved across the way because he wanted quiet. He had a life to live, and she kept getting in the way. Like old times.

It was mid afternoon when Cami finally pulled into her driveway. The heavy overcast sky swooped low and matched her pensive mood. She entered through the side kitchen door, tossing her purse and canvas tote onto the counter. Once out of her boots she glanced around for Gavin, but when she didn't see him she rushed upstairs.

In case Danny was sleeping, she padded quietly down the carpeted hallway. The master bedroom, big and lonely these past few years stood to her left, its door shut against troubled memories. Her son's room stood opposite. About to enter, she heard chatter and halted. She peeked inside. Gavin sat on the edge of her little one's bed where he rested under his blue downy comforter.

"How's your throat and tummy, chief?"

"A little better. The ginger ale you gave me helped. Where's my mom?"

"She's zipping home, unless she's stuck in traffic, surrounded by fifty ice cream trucks."

"Fifty?" Danny rasped. "No way. Not in Kindred Lake."

"Reminds me of when I was your age and sick in bed just like you. That was the time I came pretty close to owning every ice cream factory in the world and all by a silly mistake."

"Really?"

"See partner, my throat burned like a wild forest fire. I had to take matters into my own hands. Alone in the house, I snuck into my parents room to use the phone, which I'm not advising you to do, especially if you don't like maple-walnut ice cream."

"Yuck."

"You got that right. I agree with you one hundred percent. Don't ask me why, but maple-walnut was the only flavor all those factory owners made." Gavin tucked Danny's blanket tighter around him. "Settle back against your pillow and I'll finish my story. If you want."

"Yeah. Tell me more about the ice cream."

"Sssh. I'll do the talking. You listen."

Cami leaned against the hall wall. Gavin was awesome. He'd managed to guide her ill son into bed. Considering how uncooperative a sick Danny could be, that was a feat and a half. And what was up with this storytelling? Like her son, she wanted to listen and learn more about this mysterious ice cream. Actually, the more she was with Gavin the more she wanted to hear whatever he had to share. He was opening doors to safer, kinder places.

"Boy, oh boy," Gavin continued. "Every ice cream factory owner I talked to acted like a plain old grouch."

Danny giggled at the word grouch.

Cami smiled. Way to go, Gavin.

"Hey, chief, why don't you close your eyes while I finish my story."

"Don't want to."

"With your eyes closed, you'd be able to picture exactly what I'm about to tell you—like you're watching TV."

"Okay."

"Ice cream delivered to the house sounded like heaven to me, especially since our refrigerator was empty of the treat. Imagine being out of ice cream?"

Silence.

"Danny?"

"Hmm."

"The first grouch—I mean, factory owner—I talked to went on and on about how his kids hid his socks, how the dog ate his toast that his wife burned because she had to mop up the coffee the cat knocked over... Hey, chief? Are you listening?"

Silence.

"Good. You and I both need to rest."

The door creaked open. Gavin entered the hallway, dressed in a navy blue pullover sweater with a denim shirt collar poking out, and black jeans. But, it was the western-style boots that snagged her attention. He was Attraction with a capital A. She fingered her blouse collar as a little flutter zinged through her.

With a flap of his arms, he gestured surrender. "Caught me."

"Yes. But, if you help Danny fall asleep that easily, I'll consider hiring you."

"It wasn't me, but unfortunately his little spike in temperature."

She looked past his shoulder into the bedroom. "I better go and see."

"The sitter gave him the fever remedy you left directions for. He's sleeping heavily."

"One fast check," she whispered and tiptoed inside her son's room. Danny felt warm to touch, but not burning. She kissed his forehead. A little snore rolled from his mouth. She pulled the blanket up to his chin and slipped out of the room.

"Would you like a cup of coffee?"

"Sure, if it's not trouble with you fresh home from work."

"It'll be fine. Let's go into the kitchen." She had to admit it was nice to have an adult to chat with. No, that wasn't quite it, and she knew this. She talked with adult co-workers five days a week. What differed was his way of igniting her insides like sparklers in the darkest of nights. She was schoolgirl giddy.

"Have a seat," she said over her shoulder. Nervous, she blanked out where she usually kept the coffee filters. Launching a massive search for the box, she opened and closed the cabinet doors, banging them with a little extra gusto.

His hand on her shoulder stilled her. "Anything is fine. Hot chocolate or plain tap water. I'm not fussy."

She turned, and was immediately wrapped in his arms. Her breath hitched. When had he moved this close? She hadn't aimed to be in this position, but she sure did like his embrace, intentional or not.

He flashed a smile that instantly pushed the day's cold away. "If my presence here isn't a good idea, I can leave you to your privacy."

"Have a seat. Stay." Her tone came out choppy. The nervous flutter was back and bounced inside her chest like a rabbit on caffeine. She stepped aside, away from his warm and supportive hold. She tried to cover up her shakiness by filling the teakettle. "Cocoa it is."

He sat at the far end of the table. She slid onto a chair near the oven.

In need of occupying her twitchy hands, she reached for the

cloth placemat before her, and traced an old stain with a fingertip. Why wasn't he looking around the room, commenting about her antique tin collection that lined the shelves, or comparing the similar architecture of their two houses, especially their kitchens, or pick-a-topic to fill the gap between them? Instead, the last of the tension lines across his forehead unfurled. He leaned back into his chair and peered into her eyes.

This was Gavin Kinkaid looking at her.

Yes. Gavin. But definitely not the boy of years ago. And she wasn't the same girl of yesterday either.

The kettle clanked and hissed.

He reached across the table and patted her hand. "Relax. I'll fix the drinks."

Her mouth went slack. She swiped a finger slowly over her jaw hoping he didn't notice. "That's okay. You're the..." She'd stumbled over the word *guest*. He appeared comfortable enough that a stranger observing might have believed he belonged in her home, not elsewhere, separated from her.

She swallowed hard. "You're the guest," she said, managing to complete her sentence.

"And you're home from work, probably either tired or rightly frazzled about Danny. Let me take care of things. I mean, as long as you don't expect me to produce marshmallows from my sleeves, we're good."

She grinned. "If you can accomplish marshmallow magic, definitely stay. Sadly, I'm certain we're out of what Danny calls the white gooey stuff."

He placed a steaming mug before her. The sweet chocolate scent wafted toward her and she sighed her appreciation.

"Enjoy," he said and sat. He moved his chair closer. His eyes twinkled with a mischievous sparkle. "I'm certainly enjoying this moment."

She nodded. Not much seemed to upset him. He knew his way around a kitchen better than she did. Plus, he enjoyed children. Hold on, there. Why was she mentally ticking off a list of pluses about him? She sipped her drink, the sweet chocolate smoothing the last of her jitters.

"I'm enchanted by the ice cream tale you shared with Danny. How were you going to work in the maple-walnut part? And how did you know my little guy despised that flavor?"

"Show me a kid who confesses preferring maple-walnut over another flavor and I'll divulge to the world I don't make my own tomato sauce."

She shot him a playful wide-eyed look. "Since you like to cook, I guess that's the equivalent."

"In regards to the rest of the ice cream story, beats me. I'd hoped Danny would conk out by the time I came to the end. He's a great boy, Cami. I hope he feels better quickly."

"Thanks. I try my best to give him all my love. He usually rebounds fast."

"Every child needs a plentiful supply of TLC."

She nodded. "I admire your passion for helping children. Is your volunteer work at the community center linked to your counselor studies?"

"Only partially. I was involved with the national organization of Big Brothers Big Sisters when I lived in Manhattan for a couple of months before moving here. In the city the neighborhoods were a lot tougher. Kindred Lake's program sounds worthwhile to me. It doesn't matter where one lives. A broken home is a broken home. It isn't easy."

She averted her gaze. "Yes, I know."

"Looks like I stuffed my foot in my mouth again. Didn't mean to imply anything negative about your family situation."

Slowly, she lifted her gaze. The kindness in his eyes helped her to breathe easier. "No reason to be sorry. Todd's gone. You can try to sugarcoat it, but Danny is fatherless. He's from a broken home."

Gavin tapped his hot chocolate mug. "I do like kids."

"Want your own one day?" She covered her face with her hands. "I didn't mean to pry."

He pulled her hands from her face with his warm, gentle fingers. "You're not. I enjoy talking with you. You're an excellent listener."

"But this is personal, Gavin. After all those years picking on the Kinkaid name, why would you want to share private things with me, of all people?"

He squeezed her hands. "You got to stop thinking this way. I've changed. And you have too. And here's the thing." After a slight pause, he said, "You're the first person who has come along in a while that I've been able to talk with about the subject of family."

"Kind of ironic, isn't it?"

"Life's full of surprises. Daily."

"Don't I know it?"

"Yeah, I'd love to marry a good woman one day and have a child or two. Loving children and having them love you are truly miracles and gifts from God." He leaned back, but still held her hands. "But looks like God has other plans for me. I'm okay with that because I trust Him."

She studied his face. His smooth complexion tempted her to fan her fingertips across his face, to feel the masculine rise of his high cheekbones, the softness under his radiant gray-blue eyes, to smooth that one furrow line always etching his forehead. He was her type of handsome.

"Let me explain more."

"You don't have to...though I'd love to know."

"And that's why I want to share." He leaned back. "In spite of my reputation in school as the all-American bad-boy from a bad family, I managed to keep out of trouble." He winked.

She flashed him a slow smile. "Again, I love your humor."

"And I love your smile."

She pointed at herself and lifted a brow.

"Yeah. Really." He took a sip of cocoa. "I never pursued those girls from the other school that I'd been accused of dating and dumping. Weird how those rumors about my wild dating years got started since not one girl wanted to date me."

She searched his words and tone for traces of biting sarcasm, but couldn't find a drop. Gavin didn't pull the punches of retaliation or prolonging suffering. Instead, he told it like it was. She relaxed. What a comfort it was to talk and share without tension building between them.

"Then I joined the Air Force," he continued. "And met the girl of my dreams. Well, at least I thought. I loved Ariel. In my book, she was perfect."

"Your tone tells me there's an awful *but* around the corner."

He nodded. "A month after we became engaged I learned from a reliable source she was seeing another guy behind my back. At dinner that night she confessed this was true and told me of her plans to leave me. When I replied that I'd already known she turned so white I thought she was going to pass out. After she recovered, I wished her a happy life, paid the bill, and went home. Haven't seen her since, nor want to."

Cami's eyes brimmed with tears for the man whom she once scorned. And now he sat before her trusting her with his personal circumstances. "I'm sorry."

"I appreciate you listening. It feels good to tell someone about my awful almost-story."

"Is that what you meant about God's plans for you varying from your own?"

He tilted his head. "Yes and no. I'd like a family. If it happens, it will. Meanwhile, since I do enjoy kids I've volunteered with Friends. I'm the type to move on. I'll never willingly get stuck in a corner."

"I hear you about feeling crammed into a corner." Before Todd's passing she'd embraced her faith. The results were many pluses she'd never imagined before, like confidence in life turning out okay and a general sense of peace. She delighted in God's love. After Todd's death she gravitated away from Him and more toward the randomness of fate. It was as if she'd fallen into a cavern and couldn't climb out.

She glanced into Gavin's eyes. The familiar knot of turmoil and guilt twisted within her again over whether she could share about Todd.

He leaned toward her. "Anytime you need to talk, Cami, I'm here for you."

"Thank you," she said softly.

"Yeah, I admit losing Ariel wasn't fun times. But it brought me one step closer to loving God. The knowledge that I'm safe and secure in His hands is all I need. God would never turn His back on me."

"Mom!" A pajama-clad Danny staggered into the kitchen. "I don't feel good."

"Oh, honey. I'm home. I'll take care of you," she said and wrapped Danny into her embrace, reaching automatically to his forehead to check for fever.

Gavin stepped to the back kitchen door where his coat hung on a hook. "Remember, prayer always works." He opened the door. Icy cold gushed in.

"Wait," Danny called. "Will Mom and me see you again? And your puppy?"

"If you'd like."

"You bet," Danny squealed then coughed.

She patted Danny's back. "Let's get you back to bed, sweetie."

"Cami, call me," Gavin said. "Let me know how Danny is."

She looked into his awesome eyes. "Sure." She just might share a lot more.

5

"*Mom?*"

Cami glanced away from the kitchen window where she'd been sipping her coffee while watching a parade of four wild turkeys strut across the backyard on their way to the woods. Fresh on her mind was the phone call she'd received yesterday from the Friends director. Gavin had been cleared to become Danny's Friend, and now it was up to her to give the final green light.

Danny entered the kitchen wearing mismatched PJs.

"Hey, buddy. You're looking better."

"It's like I was never sick."

"I know! Two days ago you felt yucky. I'm glad you're okay now."

He sat at the kitchen table. "I want pancakes for breakfast."

Cami set her coffee mug on the counter. "Looks like your appetite's back."

"I'm starved. Make me lots, please. Maybe bacon, too."

The early morning sun sneaked past the yellow curtains over the sink, helping to brighten both the room and her mood. Yet, cooking a big meal on a Saturday failed to rate as fun. "How about oatmeal?"

Danny rubbed his nose. "That's stinky like Gavin's maple-walnut ice cream."

She laughed and considered her options. If she practiced frugality, without too much splurging, her income helped to keep them far from suffering. But today, with her son's returned health, was a day meant for a treat. "Let's go to Rick's Diner, but you'll have to bundle up. Deal?"

Her little boy flashed a smile. "Deal. They have the bestest breakfasts."

"Be dressed in five minutes and we'll leave."

"Two minutes, Mom," he shouted and scrambled out of the room then upstairs.

Her thoughts drifted back to Friends. Would Danny be willing to continue attending since his former Friend had moved? Would she be willing to allow Danny and Gavin to team up? She needed to come to a conclusion fast. Come Monday, the group would begin the preparation for the annual holiday festivities by making decorations for the store windows along Main Street. Last year, Danny enjoyed decorating the downtown merchants' windows. He'd dropped less than subtle hints since midsummer about looking forward to this year's activities. She'd try to get a feel for things better over breakfast.

*F*or a cold Saturday morning, Rick's Diner hummed with a dining room packed with chatty customers. Just after they were seated in a booth, a waiting line formed.

Danny glanced about the eatery decorated with framed newspaper articles and photographs of town history. "We came just in time."

Cami nodded, thankful for the coffee the waitress, Jacey,

poured into her mug. She had to hand it to Jacey. A woman only a few years younger than she, Jacey also was a single-mom, her adorable four-year-old son the joy of her heart.

Cami lifted her full cup, the breakfast brew wafting upward and making her smile. "How's Caleb?"

Jacey whipped out her cell phone and flashed a photo of her little boy. "Just awesome. He's so looking forward to Christmas. I am too." She slipped the phone into her apron pocket and looked over her shoulder, but not before Cami caught a furtive look in her eyes. "Got to go. With the holiday crowd picking up, Rick's on patrol."

"You keep loving that son of yours and all will be fine."

"You got that right." Jacey smiled at Danny. "Are you counting the days until Santa visits?"

"Kind of," Danny said.

"I hope so. It's a time for all kinds of surprises. I'll be back in a few minutes for your orders." Jacey disappeared into the crowd of hungry patrons.

Cami opened the menu to see what looked appealing, but the food offerings faded as Jacey's words swirled before her. *All kinds of surprises.* Cami hoped for only good, kind ones for both of them.

"Oh, cool." Danny slid out of his booth.

"Where are you going?"

"I see Gavin. He's waiting in line. I'm gonna ask him to sit with us." He made a beeline to the waiting crowd before she could reply.

Danny returned in a flash, tugging at Gavin's hand. "Mom, Gavin says he'd be *delighted* to join us. I can't remember anyone telling us they'd be delighted to be with us."

She cradled her coffee mug. "Want to join us, though no one else ever wanted to?"

Gavin grinned. "Absolutely. Everyone else is batty for turning down your company." He slipped into the booth on the opposite side, but well within arm's reach.

Danny scooted beside him. Man and child certainly made a happy-looking pair. The conclusion that Gavin and her son were already friends shouted boldly—and sweetly—in her mind. Then why the hesitation over becoming buddies at Friends?

"It's almost Christmas," Danny stated, excitement bubbling in his voice.

Gavin smiled at Danny. "What are you hoping Santa will bring?"

Danny peered around the busy eatery. In a hushed voice, he said, "Don't tell my friends I believe in Santa. I mean, I really believe in God, but Santa's cool."

"It's awesome you believe in God."

"Uh-huh," Danny said, eyeing Gavin. "Mom doesn't pray much anymore. She should. Awesome things might happen for us like another dad for me."

Cami clunked the empty mug down on the table, a bit on the loud side. She needed to cool a flush racing to her face. "Danny, may I have a sip of your water?"

Danny reached for his glass but knocked it over. She grabbed additional paper napkins from the metal holder next to the salt and pepper shakers to blot the spill.

"Still want to dine with us, Gavin?" she muttered.

"Without a doubt."

The three of them ordered their breakfasts without other spills or damages. When Jacey set their plates before them, Danny appeared pleased Gavin's order of pancakes with a side of sausage matched his. They both teased Cami about her healthier order of oatmeal and fruit salad. She enjoyed listening to the chatter between the two guys, the conversation flowing naturally as if they've been best pals for years. Her son beamed, obviously basking in the fatherly-friend attention that Gavin offered.

Fatherly-friend? Hmm.

"Let's say grace," Gavin said. He reached for their hands.

Joy rushed into Cami's heart when her son flashed the warmest smile she'd seen on him in awhile.

Gavin led them in a short but lovely prayer of thanksgiving for their food and for leading him to Cami and Danny, good neighbors and friends.

Right. Good neighbors. Good friends. She shouldn't be thinking anything more.

"A sweet grace, thank you," she said.

"I never say a word I don't mean." He looked at his dish. "Hello breakfast, my friend."

Danny laughed around a mouthful of pancake. "Mom, are you going to let go of Gavin's hand? He wants to eat."

She stared at the physical link to Gavin, and noted how her hand had quickly turned from cold to warm in his hold. Slowly, she released her grip and watched him cut into his three-stack of pancakes.

After lots of talk and gobbling, Danny set his fork down. "I'm full."

Cami looked at the half of pancake left on his dish. "Good job, hon."

"Mom, can we take a walk before we drive home? It's not cold out."

"You're right. It's not a bad day for December. Let's make the walk a short one, though."

"Okay. Can Gavin come along?" Instead of waiting for a reply, Danny faced his pal. "Mom won't embarrass us guys."

Gavin looked her way. "Promise to be on your best behavior?"

"Maybe." Teasing them both, she rolled her eyes before sliding out from the navy blue vinyl bench seat. She looked forward to this spontaneous walk with her neighbor and exuberant son. Danny was correct. It certainly was a mild day, considering the storm they had yesterday. She glanced at the man who had joined them for breakfast, one who had made her hum inside. It was truly a sunny, bright day.

"*Y*ou guys are slowpokes," Danny called over his shoulder. He sped ahead.

"Stay where I can see you, buddy." Cami glanced to her right at Gavin. "Enjoy breakfast?"

"Best pancakes I've had in a long time." He adjusted his movie star-handsome sunglasses. "But..."

She playfully lifted a brow. "Yeah?"

"Well, I do have this rep for whipping up the best chocolate chip pancakes. You and Danny will have to come over sometime and check it out for yourselves."

"To make sure your culinary standing isn't endangered?"

He pursed his lips and narrowed his gaze. "Exactly," he said, in the most serious tone she'd heard from him yet.

She laughed. "Do you cook without chocolate?"

"Is that a valid objection?"

"Got me on that one. Sure. You're on for those pancakes."

They rounded the corner and she glanced up at Gavin. She liked that their heights complemented each other. "Are you happy you're living back in Kindred Lake? Or are bad associations ruining things for you?"

"It's odd. Yes and no. And then there's the family thing." He rubbed the back of his neck. "I get that people change. Tough to imagine, but that also means my family."

"I hear what you're saying about change and family, Gavin. Look at us—we used to pray. Used to read Danny Bible stories at night, used to attend church, used to do a lot of things that have now slipped into past tense."

"And you personally?"

She stopped mid-step on the snowy sidewalk. "Like you said, we've all changed."

"Hey, Mom?"

She glanced ahead.

Danny stood before a small market and deli. "I think we need tonight's dessert."

She smiled in appreciation of the reminder, hoping to mask the sadness accosting her heart. "Thanks, big guy. I'd be lost without you."

"You're not lost, Mom. Not when Gavin and I are with you."

Gavin and I.

Sometimes children were stronger than their parents, and were able to bounce back onto their feet despite tough times. Danny was way ahead of her. She still needed to wrap her mind around this whole concept of leaving the past behind.

"Cami?" Gavin inched closer. He was going to hug her. Her breath hitched. Their gazes locked and for a sweet moment she was swept into a time of no regrets. She leaned toward him.

He pulled back and jammed his fists into his pockets. A look of doubt flashed across his expressive face. What shook her more was a sense of disappointment that he'd changed his mind. Well, that is, if he was going to hug her. It was probably her imagination.

Or her desire.

"Can I stay outside?" Danny asked.

Gavin jutted his chin at the shop. "Go inside. I'll watch Danny for you."

"I'll be right out." She trusted him with her son. The funny thing was, in watching over Danny, he was safeguarding her as well. She'd become accustomed to being the one who protected. She hadn't slipped into that position by choice, but had managed very well these past few years and hadn't thought twice. A loving mom had to do what loving moms did, and to the best of her abilities. Now, not only was Gavin back in town but also becoming someone who her son could count on. She liked what was happening. It was a nice feeling, and these days, *nice* was rare, an emotion that long ago she'd never again expected to own.

Five minutes later, with a bag full of fresh baked bread and donuts, Cami stepped outdoors. Across the street, in a public play area beside the lake, Gavin and her son flung snowballs at each other. Although she could tell they were enjoying themselves, she needed to get Danny home to rest.

The brilliant blue sky boosted her sense of serenity. She had a good home and Danny's health had improved. And a decent neighbor. Life was okay. She breathed in deep. If only it would stay good.

"Play with us, Mom," Danny shouted. Rather than wait for her reply, he tossed another snowball at Gavin, hitting him on the shoulder. "That's what you get for making goo-goo eyes at Mom! Surprised you, huh?"

In contrast to the chilly December temperature, a pleasant heat spread within Cami.

Gavin strode over. He took the grocery bag from her. "It's all good."

And it was. About to tell him she was the most comfortable she'd been with anyone in a while, Danny's waving at another boy snagged her attention.

"There's Ethan," Danny said. "He has a sled. Can I play with him?"

Cami's neck muscles tightened. *Bad News Ethan.* The boy might come from a good family and achieve good grades, but he manipulated the other kids to go along with his commands. If he said jump, the other children obeyed without hesitation. Everything connected to the boy conjured up a dangerous, way too familiar scenario right out of her past.

"You were just ill, hon. Let's go home."

"Oh, please, Mom. Just for a few minutes."

Gavin pointed to a bench. "We can keep an eye on them from there."

She supposed no harm could come from the two playing together within full view. Perhaps Danny would have a positive influence on Ethan. The boy needed a good role model. "Okay. Fifteen minutes tops, then we'll leave."

Danny agreed and hurried off.

"There's a candidate for the Friends program if I've ever seen one," she said and sat beside Gavin on the bench. She didn't move away when he inched closer, pressing warmth between them.

"Why's that?"

"Ethan's father, Steve Mathers, is always working. Remember him from school?"

Gavin pulled at his chin. "Faintly."

She averted her gaze. "He was one of the bullies, the one who wore that silly pirates cap with a matching belt, as if he was really cool and tough. It was incredible that he was never the one who others picked on."

"Oh. Right. Haven't thought about him in years."

"From what I've heard he seldom turns out for events Ethan's involved in, whether it's family functions or on a social level like the bowling team his son is on."

"Is it a case of not wanting to?"

Gavin was sharp. She liked that about him. "I'm thinking so."

"Does the kid have brothers or sisters?"

She nodded. "That's another sad issue. His younger brother has heart problems and is either in the hospital or being tended to by their mother."

"Sounds like Ethan spends a lot of time by himself when not in school."

The boy reminded Cami of their own class ringleader, Jimmy. "He's a lone wolf, but when he calls others to follow they do."

"What are the chances of Ethan checking out a Friend session?"

"Don't know. The family keeps to themselves. I used to have Ethan's brother as a student until he became ill. I haven't seen him, Ethan or their mother in a long time."

"We can have Danny invite Ethan for one day. A community group like Friends can help misguided, lonely children like Ethan."

She nodded. "Good idea. And I'll try reaching out to Ethan's mom again."

A smile lit his face. It made his grayish-blue eyes shine. Surprise fluttered within her like a butterfly enjoying a warm spring day—she enjoyed looking at him.

"You're sparkling, Cami."

"Funny, I was just thinking the same about you. I like how you have hope for the other person that no one else thinks twice about."

He playfully slugged her arm. "It's not always easy, kiddo. God wants me to turn the other cheek. Who am I to argue?"

"To love one's enemies?"

He grasped her hands. "I've always thought God plants certain people in our paths for a reason. Lately, I've stopped trying to figure out the *why* part. He is way ahead of me."

She squeezed his hand. "And that's the exact reason why I'm giving my permission for you and Danny to become Friends."

He beamed a smile. "I was hoping you'd say that."

Only after arriving home did she think twice about her own motivations for Danny at Friends. While her son would always be her first priority, she had to admit that by allowing Danny to partner with Gavin she'd also have more opportunities to see her neighbor who was fast becoming a friend.

Maybe more?

As she sorted through the pile of DVDs for them to watch that afternoon, doubt slashed through her little daydream of getting better acquainted with Gavin. He was only interested in her son because he was developing his professional image on his way to becoming a child counselor. Her little boy was simply one more notch on his list of qualifications. Plus, it was probably his faith that dictated him to forgive her, his former enemy. That was all.

6

The quiet in Gavin's house usually provided the ideal surroundings he'd dreamed about before moving back to town. Today was a whole different story. Peace and he weren't seeing eye-to-eye. His thoughts swirled around Cami, not allowing an escape route. The reality was, he wasn't looking for one.

Four hours ago he's come close to pulling her into his embrace. He wanted to hold her tight, to chase away the cold, hurting spot he suspected still gnawed away at her heart. She wasn't fragile, in need of someone to protect her. Just the opposite. Strong, brave, determined were descriptions that readily crossed his mind about her. But, as far as he could see, everyone needed help in chasing away the loneliness of living in this big world.

And he did too.

Yet, he was the one who'd pulled back from the hug when a distinct niggling voice taunted him. *She's the one who hurled insults at you and your family. She wanted nothing to do with you. You can't forgive her.*

Nonsense.

She wasn't the Camille he'd known years ago. That yesterday's girl was a different person than the woman she'd become. He'd told her that. Apparently, he needed another dosage of forgive and forget.

The doorbell rang, banishing Cami from his mind. For now, at least.

He placed the textbook onto his cluttered desk. Great timing. He wasn't fooling anyone but himself in thinking he was studying. Not with his thoughts roaming over his lovely green-eyed neighbor. And lovely she was. Yeah, both physically and personality wise. And this was the problem. Her magnetic appeal lured him to her with a powerful pull he needed to tamp down before he passed the point of no return. For both of their sakes.

He opened the door. Big mistake. The woman…the beautiful woman in question, stood right before him. And he'd thought to *tamp down* his attraction toward her? Really?

Bundled in a short gray felt jacket, a gray, white, and blue scarf held securely by a large candy cane pin, a gray knitted hat, and a wide smile, she appeared as a true holiday treat. "I'm glad you're home."

"Hi, there." Over her shoulders he saw Danny kicking the piles of plowed snow wedged against the sidewalk. "What's up?" Hmm. That wasn't his most charming line.

Her smile faltered then disappeared. He wanted to bring it back. ASAP.

"Oh, I guess I caught you at a bad time."

"Nah. I'm a bit rusty in etiquette. Excuse my caveman charisma." He stretched his shirt collar from his neck as he grasped for levity. He wanted to make her happy and blinked at this lightbulb moment. "And to think I'd pegged you as a chocoholic, one who would never veer toward candy canes."

She glanced down at the pin on her scarf then broke out in a laugh. The trill of her laughter reminded him of good times on a summer day. He could sure use warmth.

"Yeah, well, it is the holiday season."

"Red and white are nice colors on you."

She tilted her head. A little smile lifted her lips. Those stunning lips.

"Danny grew too restless to relax with a movie. So, we're heading to the library for new reading material. Want to tag along? Since you'll be paired up as Friends on Monday it would be a good idea to, uh, you know..."

"See how compatible we are outside the snowball-tossing arena?" he offered.

"Exactly."

"There you are."

She raised a brow.

"The Cami who I enjoyed breakfast with earlier—the confident Cami."

"Like that version better?"

"Without a doubt."

She pointed a finger at him, chest height. "And there you are."

He wanted to playfully grab it and tug her toward him. Maybe only inches separated them, but suddenly it was way too much distance. "Me?"

"Yep. The cheerful, easy-going guy I enjoyed breakfast with earlier." Before he could reply, she pointed to her red and white striped boots. "Like these too?"

"Keeping the candy theme is your thing." He grinned. "A nice thing."

"A spontaneous yard sale purchase back in the fall."

"That's my type of fun."

"Which? Holiday boots, yard sales, or the art of spontaneity?"

"All three."

She laughed wildly; the sweet singsong tickled his heart. He chorused her with boisterous laughter. When was the last time he'd laughed so hard, so easily?

They simmered and stared, their glazes locked on each other

like concertgoers holding their breath in wait for the next note of a Beethoven sonata.

She adjusted her scarf. "I can't imagine you wearing red and white boots."

"You never know." He waggled his brows. "If it makes you laugh, it's worth it."

She glanced over her shoulder. "I don't know how much longer his patience will last."

"I'd love to go to the library with you two. Let me give Happy a bit of puppy chow and I'll be right out."

A few minutes later the three strolled down the street. His steps were light, his pace comfortable. Who would have thought?

"My dad worked at the post office," Danny said, eying Gavin. "He was a supervisor."

"Wow. A postmaster."

"Yeah. That's what I mean."

"At which branch? The big one downtown or one of the smaller ones?"

Danny grinned. "The biggest. Because Dad was good at his job. Super good."

"Honey?" Cami, trailing behind a few feet, stepped up. "Are you bragging?"

Danny hesitated, fidgeting with his lime-green ski hat. "No. Just miss him."

She pulled him into a hug. "I know you do. Your dad loved you so much. I also know you're making him proud."

"I am?"

"You sure are. And you're making me proud too."

Gavin's gut clenched. This talk couldn't be easy for either mom or son. He grasped her hand and gave it a little squeeze.

She glanced at their hands then at Danny and back at their woven fingers. She stepped aside and again wrapped an arm around her son, but he pulled back.

"It's okay, Mom. I miss Dad, but like you tell me, that's

normal." Danny looked his way. "Since you're not in the Air Force anymore, what do you do for work?"

"I came close to making a career in the military, but decided to help children by becoming a counselor. Presently, I'm a full time college student."

Danny's mouth dropped open. "You mean you want to go to school when no one is making you?"

He chuckled. "Believe me, I can't wait until I graduate."

"When will that be?" Cami asked.

"This May."

"Cool," Danny said.

Cami nodded. "Yes, way cool."

He put a hand on Danny's shoulder. "It doesn't bother you that your new Friend isn't a construction worker or a hotshot business man or into sports?"

"No way. Mom always tells me to respect people."

"Your mom is teaching you well." He flashed a smile at Cami. "You rock."

Danny giggled. "Mom does rock. She's the best."

A tear meandered its way down Cami's cheek. She turned away, but Gavin was able to read her thoughts. Respecting others. Or not. The phantom of guilt was making an appearance. The past difficulties stood between them as sorely as a cell tower built between two scenic hills. There was something more, though. A heavy-duty item, for sure. He scratched the side of his head in wonder.

"Can we take a shortcut to the library?" Danny asked. "I'm getting tired."

Cami pulled up Danny's jacket zipper. "And you're probably cold. Silly me for agreeing on a walk only a few days after you've been sick."

"You're not silly, Mom. I like walking. Besides, there's this neat house I want to show you. My friends and me like to pretend it's a haunted house. It looks like no one lives there."

She huffed out a heavy breath. "On this street?"

"A haunted house?" Gavin mused aloud.

"You gotta see it," Danny said. "It's messy with a lot of stuff around it."

Gavin faced Cami and shrugged. "I think God's telling us it's time to deal with our past, after all." He looked Danny right in the eyes. "I know the house, chief. My folks live there. That's where I grew up."

Danny's mouth dropped open. "They still live there? Way cool."

Gavin snagged a quick look at Cami. Worry draped across her face like a dusty cloak.

We'll see how cool it is, Danny. We'll see.

❄

Whatever little control Cami had on life frizzled before her eyes. Her son had unintentionally placed her and Gavin in a situation she would've done most anything to avoid.

The raggedy late nineteenth century house came into view. Gavin and she slowed in pace. Danny raced ahead and bumped his hand along the weathered wooden fence lining the front yard. About to tell him to respect others' property, the words tripled in weight on her tongue. The front door squeaked open. Beth Kinkaid stepped onto the porch. Dressed in a white turtleneck sweater, winter-white slacks, and a knee-length black sweater, the colors enhanced her silvery hair and slim figure. She looked warm and relaxed, and lovely as ever.

Cami stiffened. She hoped she didn't look as tense as she felt.

"It will be okay." Gavin squeezed her hand. "I'll make sure this goes well."

She nodded. Trust. Between the two of them. A nice thing.

"Gavin, what a pleasant surprise," Beth called. Her face

glowed in joy. She opened her arms. "Come give me a hug."

Without a delay, Gavin bounded up the porch steps. He wrapped his mom in an embrace. When they pulled apart she smiled warmly at Cami and Danny.

"What a delight to see you two. Welcome."

"Hello, Mrs. Kinkaid," Cami said.

"If you're with my son then it's for pleasure. Please call me Beth."

"Nice sweater, Mom," Gavin said. "But you'll freeze without a coat on."

"Not when I have my son home to warm my heart." She glanced again at Cami and Danny. "Would your friends like to join us inside? I already know Danny and it's about time I get to know his mom better. Those parent-teacher conferences don't encourage much personal exchange."

Words escaped Cami. While she felt relief that Gavin's mom regarded her not so much as a parent of one of her pupils but more a friend, nervousness still plagued her. Surely Beth was just being polite with her invitation to come into her home when what she likely desired was for them to leave her family alone. Would Beth finally confront her about those yesteryears now that they were on the Kinkaid home turf rather than at school? Cami glanced at her son with his eager listening ears, and all the respect and trust in his mom to lose.

Danny stomped snow from his boots. "Can we go inside, Mom? Mrs. Kinkaid's nice. You'll like her. I never thought she'd be the one who lives in this run-down place."

Cami gasped, her son's name snared in her mouth. She braced for a scowl to cross Beth's face. Instead, the older woman smiled and waved her hands outward in invitation.

"Danny," Beth said. "We're grateful to have our humble home. Let's go indoors for hot drinks. If you enjoy hot cocoa, I have a fresh bag of marshmallows and real whipped cream in the fridge."

Danny rubbed his belly. "Yum. I love cocoa. And real whipped cream."

Gavin glanced at Cami. "Whatever you'd like to do, I'm game."

Other than hide? Gooseflesh pricked Cami's arms. She thought about the WWJD bracelets popular some years back. She inhaled a deep, calming breath. "A visit sounds great. Thanks for the invitation, Beth. And please call me Cami."

Beth pointed to the porch doormat. "Please wipe your boots. I rather play with my grandkids or volunteer at the Red Cross than spend my time mopping floors."

As Cami climbed over the missing step onto the porch, she gave Beth's words consideration. She thought about her parents' house. There were better things to do in life than keep a sterile, clean home. She might learn a lesson or two from this woman. She exchanged a smile with Gavin. He held the door for her and together, they walked into a dark hallway.

"This part of the house was built in 1889," Beth said. She continued to lead them down the corridor past dusty cardboard boxes and a couple of antique glassed-bookcases. "The kitchen wing got tacked on in 1910, in September of that year, to be exact."

"I adore old homes," Cami said. "You're fortunate to know the dates."

"It helps that the house was kept in the family."

"Wow. You're doubly fortunate."

Beth nodded. "Yes, we are."

Despite the clutter of phone directories, stacks of tied newspapers bound for recycling, and various mysterious piles Cami couldn't discern, the large kitchen caught her fancy. The round claw foot oak table stood proudly in the center of the room, centered over a pink and purple braided rug. Unlike her own kitchen table, Beth's was free from junk accumulation; only one napkin holder that looked as if it were crafted by hand centered the tabletop.

"My big project in seventh grade shop class," Gavin said,

reading her mind.

Beginning to relax, Cami felt as comfortable as if she were in her own kitchen. Definitely an unexpected reaction.

Beth gestured toward the table. "Have a seat. I'll have those hot drinks ready in no time. You're in luck. My youngest daughter baked us a pumpkin strudel coffee cake and dropped it off this morning on her way to work." She beamed a radiant smile. "My children make me proud."

"Oh, you don't have to fuss on account of us."

"I'd like to. Gavin's home, and with friends."

"And I love pumpkin," Danny said.

Cami chuckled. "Danny, you like anything sweet."

Gavin leaned toward her ear. "So do I." Louder, he added, "My sister's a fabulous baker. You'll have major regrets if you don't sample a slice."

Her heart thumped, and this time she was sure it wasn't over the offer of cake. "Well, coming from you, I'll have to trust your opinion. You know the way around an oven much better than I do."

Beth paused beside the stove. "Sounds like you know my son well, Cami. Who would have imagined years ago Gavin would enjoy baking, children, let alone join the Air Force?"

"Mom," Gavin said with a playful scolding tone. "I'm not a bill of goods to sell."

"Son, you're a woman's dream come true. And I'm a proud mama."

He covered his face, but peeked through splayed fingers. "Cami, let me re-introduce my mom, the matchmaker."

Cami bounced up. "Where are my manners? How can I help?"

Beth pointed at Cami then the chair. "Sit. Relax." She fixed her attention on her son.

"Your pop and I were hoping you'd visit much sooner than today."

"I closed on the house the end of November then kept busy

with moving." Gavin stood and took the tray of hot drinks from his mom and carried them to the table.

Beth followed with the cake and paper plates. "Hope you don't mind me not using the Sunday best."

"This is fine," Cami said. "Practical."

"Yes. Practical we are. We Kinkaids are proud but not stuffy. We love each other more protectively than a mama bear with her cubs." Beth took a seat beside Gavin and reached for his hand. "That's why Pop and I don't understand about you staying away, especially since it's been a while since your last visit. I'm aware of the friction between you two, but still…"

Gavin, who had just plopped a few marshmallows from the bag into his steaming mug, pushed the drink aside. "Where is the mighty Kinkaid anyway?"

"At the garage."

"But it's Saturday."

"Do you go to church, Mrs. Kinkaid?" Danny asked.

Cami blinked at the non sequitur question. "Please don't interrupt. And, honey, that's a personal question. We've talked about asking things like that."

Beth sipped her drink then placed the dark blue mug down on the fabric placemat. "Danny dear, no. We don't go to church. Out of this large clan Gavin is the only one who attends. My husband has his business to run and he's working on poor old Mrs. Hibbolt's car that is as ancient as she is. He's a bit behind. Probably will work more tomorrow, even if it's Sunday. He should be home within a few minutes though, for a late lunch."

"You don't believe in God?" Danny pressed.

Cami rested a hand on her son's shoulder. "Enough questions. Please."

"It's okay," Beth said. "Believe me, I'd be upfront if it wasn't."

"She would indeed," Gavin mumbled.

Beth sliced a piece of cake each for Cami and Danny. "We used to attend church once upon a time." The way Beth eyed

Gavin led Cami to believe the woman was silently asking him if she should continue. His noncommittal expression again set off alarm bells in Cami's mind. She and Danny shouldn't have stepped foot into the Kinkaid's home.

"You're like us," Danny said. "We stopped going to church right after my dad died."

Cami grasped Danny's hands.

Beth cut a piece of the coffee cake and set the dish onto her placemat. She didn't sample the cake. "I very much believe in God. I would like for my family to attend church like we used to when the children were young." She leaned her palms against the table's edge. "These past years my husband has been shaking a fist at God because of how our family was treated when the kids were young."

Danny's eyes widened. "Someone wasn't nice to them?"

Cami held her breath. A slow burn clawed its way down toward her belly.

"I'm afraid so. Rocks were thrown through our windows. Our children came home from school in tears because of insults from the neighborhood children."

Danny fingered his fork. "Why were they mean?"

"They saw us as different. My husband didn't like to hear church sermons about loving each other while we were picked on by others."

Danny wiggled in his seat. "My mom says to treat everyone nicely."

"Interesting advice, all considering," a deep, raspy voice said.

Everyone turned toward the side kitchen door. A cold breeze whipped through the open door where a slightly shorter duplicate of Gavin stood with crossed arms. His hair was more silver than Cami had last seen years ago. And though he and his son might have shared the same tint of grayish blue eyes, the older Kinkaid's were frostier.

He slapped the door shut. "Son, 'bout time you're home.

We've missed you."

"Cami and Danny," Beth said. "This is my husband, Gavin's pop, Jake."

Gavin stood and extended a hand toward his father. Jake pushed it aside and pulled him into a huge bear hug followed by pats on the back.

"Pop, this is—"

Jake cemented his gaze on Cami. "I know exactly who Ms. Hitchcock is."

"Pop, stop. It's Cami Richardson, not at all the little girl—"

Jake pursed his lips. "I think you're the one who needs to stop the nonsense, son."

Cami swallowed hard. Her sentence had just been cast. Cami, guilty of helping the neighborhood children to denounce and harass the Kinkaid family. Cami, guilty of not putting an end to the wrong. Cami, once a first-class loser, always a loser.

"Excuse me," Jake said. "After I wash off this car grease from my hands, I have to log onto the Net and see whether I can find myself an old car part for a '66 Pontiac I'm working on."

Danny grinned widely. "Wow, cool, Mr. Kinkaid. I never thought you'd have a computer in this kind of house."

Cami sprang ramrod straight. "Danny, please apologize to Mr. Kinkaid."

Jake rubbed the back of his neck. "And what kind of house would that be, young fellow?"

"This big, old house with lots of nice old things. My mom calls them an . . . anti . . ."

"Antiques," Cami said. She was grateful when Gavin squeezed her hand.

Danny nodded. "Antiques. It's hard to imagine a computer in a place with old stuff."

One by one, like dominoes knocking into the next one, laughter spread from person to person. Everyone except Jake Kinkaid. He turned his back and exited the room.

7

"*M*om, it will be okay at Friends. You'll see."

Cami smiled. Since this was Danny's first Friend meeting with Gavin, she'd left work early to pick him up from school. She'd parked the car at the Common Street lot and they walked to the community center. "I appreciate your reassurance, sweetie, though I should be the one encouraging you."

"You can trust us."

"I'm sure of that. You two certainly hit it off the other day at the library."

"And before at his folks' home."

A nervous flutter twitched her belly. She'd hoped to avoid the subject of their visit to the Kinkaid home. She and her son definitely had differing opinions of good times.

"Mrs. Kinkaid is super nice," Danny added. "Their big house is full of lots of things."

She wanted to get his mind off of the looks of the house. "They needed a large house because they raised five children."

"Like Grandma and Grandpa needed one for you and your sisters, right?"

Grateful to have arrived at the community center, she pulled open the door and followed her son into the lobby of the 1920s building.

Danny slipped off his hood. "Grandma and Grandpa's house is different from the Kinkaids' house. They're neater, not like the Kinkaids. But, Gavin's family is way happier than Grandma and Grandpa."

Evidently, there was no escaping this topic. She batted a tear back. "It's just my family's way, hon. Grandma, Grandpa, and your aunts love you. Have no doubt."

"But I don't remember when they last hugged me like Mrs. Kinkaid hugged Gavin."

She couldn't remember the last time she'd been hugged by her parents or sisters either. They gave new meaning to the words reserved and non-demonstrative. "Everyone is different, hon. People have various ways of expressing their love for each other. How about the next time you see your grandparents you hug them first?"

"Me?"

"Yes, you," she replied with gentleness in her tone.

"And you too."

"Okay. I will. They may not expect a hug or want one, but let's give them one anyway."

"Deal?" Danny asked.

"Deal."

"Cool. Wonder what Gavin would say?"

Looked like she wasn't the only one who thought about Gavin these days. "Better yet, I know God's smiling because of you. You're a wonderful boy, Danny, who will one day grow into an extraordinary man. I love you, peanut butter cup."

"Love you too, Mom." He giggled. "And I love your names for me. They make me smile inside." He grew serious. "Know what else, Mom?"

Pure goodness gleamed in his eyes and helped to dry her tears. "Yes?"

"I like this God thing happening."

She placed her hands on his shoulders. "God thing?"

"Ever since Gavin moved here it's like God is cool again. It's nice we talk about God. I missed it."

"Faith, hon. Believing in God is called having faith."

"Totally awesome, Mom. Know why?"

She lifted a brow.

"Remember when I was a kid and I drew stick figures? If we were like sticks, we'd look really shrimpy next to humongous God. There's not enough paper in the world to draw God."

"You got that right." She pulled her special boy into a hug. "And that's why we need Him. He's huge. We're tiny."

"And we live in a big world."

She nodded, too emotional to talk. *Gavin*. He was bringing back good things into their lives. God and family hugs. Couldn't go wrong.

Danny pulled away. "I'm a big boy now."

She understood, not that it made it any easier. He didn't want to be seen by his pals holding her hand. "Okay. I'll try my best to behave."

He grinned silly. "I'm proud of you, Mom."

"Thank you, sweets. Are you ready to meet your *new* Friend?"

"Yep. Let's rock 'n' roll."

She chuckled. Where did Danny pick up that expression? On second thought, she didn't want to know. Tucked under Gavin's protective, brotherly wings, her son was in good hands.

"Go ahead. I'll follow you up."

"Hey, chief." Gavin stood at the top landing. He flashed a smile at both of them. And, what a smile, one warm enough to iron out the wrinkles from a tangled day.

Danny leapt upstairs and high fived his new Friend. "Hey, Gavin."

Her son's pal pointed to the large social room behind him. "Go and say hi to the other boys and girls. I'll be right in."

"See ya later, Mom," Danny called and raced inside.

"Danny's one eager and excited boy, Cami."

His voice, a gentle lilt, vanished the cold winter temperature from her veins. His easy ways carried her off to a place where guilt, misgivings, and sorrow failed to cloud the sunny calm of peace.

"He is," she said, having reached the top step. "I have you to thank."

"Come and join us. You'd brighten the atmosphere." Gavin rubbed at the corner of his mouth rising up in a smile. "You'd brighten my day."

For the first time in years her heart beat with the unmistakable thump of hope. "Sure. I'd like to, but only for a short while. I don't want to interfere." She climbed up the stairs.

Cami stepped closer to open the door to the large recreational room, but Gavin reached out for her arm. Gently, he swung her around. They stood eye to eye. "I'm glad you trust me. I like Danny. I like you."

Had she heard a little upbeat emphasis in his tone when he said he'd like her?

Gavin, what are you doing to me?

Another thought darted through her mind. She peered heavenward. *God...what are you doing for me?* Did she deserve to have her burdened spirit lifted?

*O*n Friday, Gavin stood at the DMV table and sighed warily at the ridiculous amount of forms he needed to fill out. Like he had nothing better to do with his life. He could have easily renewed his registration through the mail weeks ago but no, procrastination ruled again. He had an ethics report due on Monday in addition to following up on a request from Danny for an additional board game at Friends.

The office door creaked open. A breeze snuck in and raced down his neck, reminding him again of the necessity to buy himself a decent coat for Pennsylvania winters. The flimsy jacket he wore didn't keep him warm enough.

"Hello, there," a melodic voice sailed through the air.

He looked up and into Cami's eyes. This time he was reminded of a grassy meadow filled with wild flowers. A happy buzz zipped through him. "You just made my day."

She exaggeratedly looked over her shoulders. "Don't tell anyone, but I'm horrible at filling out personal paperwork separate from work."

He pointed at his own stack of papers. "Believe me, you're not alone. He shoved the pile over to make room for her. "I can picture the red tape you're required to complete at Little Bears."

She stepped beside him. "Nightmare fodder, believe me."

He tried to focus on the conversation rather than her rose-scented perfume. "You must have tons of stuff to do."

"It's true what they say about teachers and supervisors—our work is never done. I think our version of homework came before we started to assign it to students."

Yet, she didn't dig into the stack of papers she'd carried in. She didn't turn away from him, either. That was okay. He liked this thing—whatever it was—happening between them. He didn't want to change a thing.

She eyed the grim-looking DMV clerk behind the counter and sighed. "Guess I'll get a number and wait my turn to ask my laundry-list of questions." Yet, instead of moving she remained beside Gavin.

He stared at the papers he'd shoved aside and whistled. "Terrific. Looks like I have the wrong forms. I'll have to get back into line." His feet were glued to the spot beside Cami. He wasn't going anywhere away from this stunning woman.

She blinked. "You go ahead since you were here first."

"No, no. You go. You probably have to rush home for Danny's bus."

"Danny's bus," she echoed. "Oh, right. Yes. Danny's bus." Rooted in place like the snowman family built in front of the motor vehicle building, Cami didn't turn away from him.

The door opened. A couple walked in and got onto the eight-person line.

"Avoiding the line isn't doing either one of us good." He hooked elbows with her, their hands touching. He wanted more. Did she?

He guided her to the line. "How has your day gone?"

"Let's just say I'm glad it's Friday."

"I walked here. Did you? We can go home together." He eyed the line. "We'll eventually get done and continue onto the next exciting chapter of our lives...like writing a grocery list."

"Funny," she cracked. Her eyes brightened. "Yes, let's go back...together." She pointed toward the window facing the curb. "I drove straight from work. I'm parked in the lot across the street. I'll give you a ride."

"Thanks. Pop has my car in the shop for an oil change and a set of new plugs."

"It must be handy having a mechanic in the family. My husband used to tinker with our cars. Now I'm at the mercy of assorted recommendations. Still trying to find a reliable one."

Gavin hated the heartbreak in Cami's tone. Wanting to make it better for her, he blocked out the fact they stood in a public building and began to pull her into his arms. He'd hold her tight, and wait for the troubling moment to pass. Too bad things weren't different between her and his pop. He knew cars better than anyone.

The clerk behind the window cleared her throat. "May I help you?"

Cami jumped back. Gavin tightened his grip reflexively.

"My turn," she whispered and stepped toward the counter.

Fifteen minutes later they walked outdoors to a biting, snapping wind at their faces. Cami pulled on her hood and pointed to her car. Within seconds they were tucked inside the vehicle. The heater blasting residual hot air quickly warmed their feet and hands.

"At least the cold temperature helps to set the Christmas mood." He rubbed his hands together for a little more warmth.

"This time of year I replay old daydreams of Christmas under a Florida palm tree." She glanced in her rearview mirror and backed out of the parking spot. "Not that I've been in a holiday mood for some time."

He followed his intuition. "Since your husband passed on?"

She tightened her grip on the steering wheel.

"I shouldn't have asked. You don't have to reply."

She shook her head. "I'm a bit weighed down. Today would have been our tenth anniversary—we were married three weeks before Christmas."

He exhaled sharply. "I can see why today—and the holiday season—is a rough one. I'm sorry for your troubles."

"I deserve it."

He went still, not wanting to believe his ears. "Nobody deserves heartbreak."

She stared at the road ahead. He wanted to respect her need for personal space and held back the dozen or so questions forming in his mind, but when she slipped her hand off the steering wheel he grasped it. He cradled her cold fingers with his warm hands. She didn't pull away. He prayed and prayed for her during the remainder of the silent trip home.

Cami turned right onto Cottage Road, drove halfway down the street then turned right into her driveway. She cut the engine and stared at the digital clock on the dashboard.

"Amazing. We actually beat the school bus by ten minutes. I thought I'd miss Danny."

"Things have an interesting way of working out at certain times."

She nodded, staring straight ahead.

"Thanks for the ride." He fumbled at the door release.

"Gavin, stay with me."

"Sure." He resettled into his seat. "You don't owe me an explanation, though. We can talk neighbor-talk if you like."

"About the weather or how the mail's delivered late on Saturdays?" She then clucked, a hybrid sound halfway between a chuckle and a snicker. "Oh, Gavin. Who would have ever thought we'd be neighbors?"

"Certainly not me as a twerpy kid."

"You were never twerpy."

"Actually Cami, I wasn't certain about lots of things and probably came across as in-your-face annoying."

"Believe me, you weren't the annoying one."

With her coat hood off, her blond hair glistened in the rare December sunlight. He couldn't resist a second longer and weaved his fingers through those luscious tresses, silk between his fingers. "What I meant to say was back in my childhood days my self-esteem hit bottom."

"Us neighborhood kids calling you names didn't help one bit." She sighed and turned away. "Unpleasant words have a way of haunting each one of us."

"Look at me, Cami. I want to see those pretty eyes. I like looking at them."

She looked downward. "I don't think I heard right."

"Yes, you did. They're the eyes of someone strong, and decent."

She faced him slowly. Sadness dragged the corners of her eyes downward.

"You must have me confused with someone else. I'm not strong, nor decent."

"Why the harsh self-judgment?"

"I was mean to you and your family, which is more than enough reason."

"You're being hard on yourself. You know, I think us becoming good neighbors is taking God's desire for us to love thy neighbor as thyself to heart. Actually, Teach, I'm thinking God's looking down upon us right now and is giving us an A plus for effort."

A little hesitant smile played with her lips, her *sweet* lips. "And your rating?"

"I forgive you." After a pause he added, "Can you forgive yourself?"

"It's not that simple." She slipped her mittens on. "Over the years I've prayed. A lot. I used to be quite a prayer warrior. Never did get around to asking God to forgive me, though. Ironic, huh?"

"I think it's sometimes easier to pray for others than it is for ourselves."

She nodded. "Definitely."

"What made you stop praying?"

The school bus hissed to a stop at the curb and flashed its red lights.

She opened the driver's door, the chance of a beginning smile long gone.

"It's my fault Todd died. How could God—or I—forgive that?"

8

*C*ami had kept the topic of her husband's last evening alive off-limits. Simply, in its own complex way, she hadn't wanted to speak about it. Not even with her parents. Although she now was tempted to share with Gavin, with the pangs of self-blame pressing down on her shoulders she wasn't ever sure where to begin. Some things were best left in the dark of silence.

After Danny's arrival home from school, Gavin had accepted her invitation indoors for a hot drink. Her son had whooped in excitement and raced them to the front door. As Gavin and she approached the house she kept glancing at her former yet forgiving enemy, now neighbor. He was Danny's official Friend, and the affable, chummy way he always was to her said something pretty wonderful about his desire to be her friend as well.

Was there something more growing between them?

She couldn't deny a second longer that this caring and *with-it* gentleman with undeniably hot looks stirred her in forgotten ways.

But now, he also knew that it was her fault her husband had died. Their tender relationship would surely turn for the worst.

While Danny changed from his school clothes upstairs, she invited Gavin to make himself comfortable in the kitchen while she lit the kettle.

"Like popcorn?" she asked with a furtive glance over her shoulder, nervous to meet his beautiful and wise eyes straight on.

If she kept busy, he wouldn't see her shaking hands.

She opened the refrigerator and grabbed a stick of butter to melt for the popcorn. *I can do this. Not a problem.* She then opened the cabinet beside the refrigerator to search for the popcorn. Not a bag in sight. Couldn't be. She always kept a plentiful stock of the kernels, especially in the wintertime.

As if her mind insisted upon focusing on this feast-your-eyes-upon man in her kitchen, she became aware he stood from his seat. And leaned against the counter. Inches away from her. Watching. Really? She swallowed hard. He was near enough to feel his warm breath on her neck. Near enough to inhale the sweet vanilla of his shampoo.

She didn't want to move.

He could easily wrap her in his arms and hold her close to his heart, a place she wanted to be tucked in and kept.

Crazy. What was she? A giddy teen girl or a mature woman? She needed to face the truth. She was a plain old neighbor. She shook her head in hope to chase away her silly daydreams.

Find the popcorn. Take all the time possible. Danny will come back into the kitchen...one of these days...and then she could dodge this confrontation or confession or whatever this lump of pain was around her heart.

"There it is," Gavin said, pointing to the popcorn right in front of her.

No more lingering for her. She reached for the bag, but it slipped from her fingers, rattling on its way to meet the floor. She scooped up the bag; too aware his gaze riveted tight on her every move. The thing that got her was that wherever his gaze landed—her hand, waist, or the small of her back—she felt the press of warmth against her skin as if he was touching her. Is that what she wanted? She swallowed hard. Heaven help her. Yes. She wanted his touch.

Slowly, she unclasped the twist tie.

He covered her hand with his. "Let me help."

Let me help.

Oh, he was. She felt safe around him. But it was more than emotional. She couldn't deny it. Even his gentle touch made her knotted muscles uncoil and helped her relax. Yet, she couldn't deny it a second more. A distinct and delicious fervor buzzed through her.

The bag's wire twister poked her palm and she jerked. The bag tumbled again to the floor, this time spilling open. White-yellow kernels spread like confetti over the green tiles.

"Oh," she squeaked. She sank to her knees beside the popcorn puddle. "What am I doing on the floor? I need the whiskbroom and dustpan." About to spring up Gavin plopped onto his knees beside her.

"It's fine," he murmured, his soft tone a caress in her ears. "I'll clean the mess."

Unable to intelligently reply, she lowered her head.

He squeezed her shoulder. "Hey, sweetheart. You're okay. Remember that."

She moved her foot and accidentally sent the kernels flying across the floor, disbanding like a bunch of thieves seeking to hide. She sighed loudly. "I can't do a thing right today—on a lot of days."

"Cami." Her name never sounded as pretty and soft from a man's lips. "Believe me, dropped popcorn does not mark you a bad person. Everything will work out for the best."

She shook her head, feeling more like a disobedient child who preferred to pout. "Not every story has a happy ending."

"The ones God writes do."

"Ohhh." The word had trailed from her mouth like a jet's wispy contrail.

He feathered his fingers across her jawbone, making her aware of her clenched teeth.

"You're tense. Go sit down—get comfortable—and let me clean this up."

"But you're the guest."

"Point me in the direction of your broom closet and forget it ever happened."

"It's over there," Danny said, plodding barefooted into the kitchen. He carried a pet cage.

Cami was outnumbered, gratefully so. Her anxiety eased.

Gavin pointed at the cage. "Who's your friend, chief?"

"Miss Mary Jane, my hamster. Just got her three days ago." Danny set the cage on the counter by the sink and glanced at Cami. "I'll get the broom. You take it easy, Mom. Together, we guys will take care of the popcorn. No big deal."

She was accustomed for being blamed when things went wrong. Well, she'd take a clue from her son and Gavin. If they weren't making a stink, she wouldn't either. It was okay, after all.

Within seconds, the kernels were deposited in the trash. Within minutes, the three of them sat around the kitchen table, sharing fresh popcorn, herbal orange tea, and hot chocolate as if it were the only natural thing to do on a December afternoon. As if Gavin belonged beside her.

Tucked in her cage, Miss Mary Jane watched them.

Gavin clasped his fingers around his mug. "Danny, tell me about your hamster. Where did you ever get a fancy name like Miss Mary Jane?"

"I wanted a puppy, especially after getting to know your doggy Happy. But Mom says hamsters make a better first pet. She says if I can take care of MJ—that's what I call her for short—then I can get a dog. Mom helped me pick out her name from a book we were reading together about an awesome woman who did nice things for others."

Gavin reached for the carafe on the snowman-shaped trivet in the center of the table and poured Cami another round of tea. "MJ is cool and cute."

"I wanted a creepy name like Lizard-guts, but Mom thought we needed a break from scary stuff that might bring our night-mares back."

Gavin lifted a brow.

"Right, Mom?" Danny began to tap on the empty ceramic bowl once full of popcorn.

Cami reached to still Danny's hands. She didn't need help in forming a headache. She had a hunch one would strike any second, unaided.

"That's not exactly what I said, but it doesn't matter. You and MJ have settled down to be quite a pair of friends." She nodded at Gavin. "Like your new Friend."

"I still want a puppy. They're fun. Dad said pets were a hassle and we couldn't have them. Sometimes, I think I got in his way too. Like I caused trouble for him."

Cami's heart cracked into pieces—and to think she'd believed they were on the rebound from Todd's passing. She enveloped Danny's hands.

"Oh, hon. I'm sorry you thought you were in your dad's way because you weren't. He loved you with all of his heart. His personal problems kept him from showing it at times."

"A lot of times." Danny pulled away from her. "Hey, Gavin. Are you in Friends 'cause your dad isn't cool with you?"

She gasped. "Danny."

A little smile dimpled Gavin's chin. "Actually, Danny, my pop is a pretty good father. We've had our moments, though, when things between us get a bit like an overcooked, bad batch of Hungarian Goulash, but we made it through without many scratches. I moved back to Kindred Lake to try to mend our relationship. I'm at Friends to help boys like you who could benefit from someone my age being a buddy because for one reason or another their dads aren't around. Besides, I like you, chief."

"You're pretty awesome too." Danny raised his hand. "Give me our secret high-five."

Gavin grinned. "Of course. But, then your mom will know our top secret rite."

"But it's only Mom."

"Thanks a lot," Cami said in mock irritation.

"But, you're cool, Mom."

"Hmm. I guess I won't share your routine with a soul." She watched the two slap an elaborate high-five. Joy heated her heart.

"Danny, I think it's time for you to excuse yourself and begin your homework. If you need help with the math part I'll poke my head into your room in a few minutes. Gavin must have his own studies to busy himself with too."

Danny sighed. "I was hoping you'd forget." He said goodbye to Gavin, then raced from the kitchen with MJ in tow.

Cami let the room simmer in needed silence for a moment. She smoothed her placemat. "Thanks, for being here, Gavin. Thanks, for being who you are."

"Never thought I'd hear those words from your mouth."

She recognized his light teasing and smiled. "And I never thought I'd say those words either. You're a special man, Gavin Kinkaid." Her gaze hooked with his, casting them together like two dance partners twirling a tango around the corners of the stars, sliding hand in hand on Saturn's rings, stepping to the same steady beat in the cosmos. She could hear a brilliant, luscious music...a Brazilian classical guitar melody. Seductive.

The possibilities playing out on the widescreen of her imagination tilted her forward.

"Do you want me to leave?" he said, his voice husky.

"No."

He grasped her hands and stroked the tops. "Is this better?"

She nodded.

"We don't have to talk. Let's enjoy the quiet a winter afternoon brings us."

A loud thunk penetrated through the kitchen ceiling. She peered upward, toward her son's room above.

"Quiet? Not in this house."

He flashed a winsome smile. "We can talk about light and insignificant things like whether you like Christmas Ribbon Candy or—"

"Or whether I've led you to believe I had shot my husband or other horror."

"You have an interesting version of light talk. I admit I'm curious about that one."

She glanced away, pulling free from his hands. Part of her wondered if she should flee, run out of the room and away from the truth that had left her empty and numb. Hadn't she mastered the art of keeping so busy the past few years that she hadn't had to deal with her agony, or the grief she'd caused? Somehow she knew it would be best to remain and to talk with this man who wanted to listen. She wanted to open up to him. Fully.

"For the record," she began, turning back to face him. "Todd crashed his car into a utility pole. He died on impact."

His mouth grew small. "How awful."

"I pushed him to that point."

He took hold of her hands again. "Tell me more."

She inhaled a deep breath and let it out slowly. "Todd had his act together when we first met. At least, outwardly. We fell in love quickly, and married quickly. Then, little by little he began to lose it, emotionally, I mean."

He touched her cheek and gently brushed away a stray tear she hadn't realized she'd shed until then.

"I chose to stay with Todd through both the rough and good times, respecting and upholding our marriage vows."

"For better or worse. That's what God wants."

She sniffled. "Oh, yes."

"Still want to share more?"

She nodded. "If you're willing to listen to this sob story."

"It's no sob story, sweetheart. You bet I want to hear what you have to say."

Sweetheart? That was the second time he'd used that endearment within a few minutes. She'd have to contemplate the word more, later, when she wasn't awestruck—or thick in the middle of the sad story that had been her marriage.

"Todd's emotional problems got the best of him. Ditto for our family life. He'd been diagnosed as clinically depressed. He should have been under a doctor's care, but he wouldn't listen to my urgings for him to get help. He didn't have a problem. The way he saw things, he was fine. I wasn't."

"Twisting reality is part of mental illness. It's like going through life with the wrong lenses on."

"Yes, believe me, I know. But, I couldn't persuade him otherwise. Unfortunately, our disagreements got out of control and became quite the heated battles. Poor Danny. He suffered his share of ups and downs. It's amazing he's not exhibiting heavy-duty problems of his own."

"Your son is a strong one. And it's because he has you as a loving mother, Cami." He wiped another renegade tear working its way down her cheek, a warm touch to her cold skin.

"Thank you," she said. She wished her words were louder, and stronger. "I needed a little bit of reassurance."

"I mean it. You're a good person. A beautiful woman."

Beautiful?

"And God was—is—watching out for you, Cami."

God. Uncertain what to think, she studied the corner of the table.

"We fought pretty badly that night. Thank goodness Danny was at a friend's overnight birthday party. For weeks, Todd had threatened that if I pressured him once more to see a doctor he'd take things into his own hands. You know, do himself in. Back then I thought he yelled those harsh words out to rattle me. The reality was it got the best of him and robbed his life."

"Todd combined suicide threats with the wrongful arguments you were pushing him to the brink of destruction."

Gavin was a good listener. "You got that right." Cami paused, but decided to press right into the thick of it. "I kind of lost it that night, as well. I told him to leave, and he did. Forever. The authorities weren't able to tell whether Todd intentionally crashed or whether it was a tragic, accidental death. I take responsibility of his death and our son losing his dad. Looking back, Todd cried out for help plenty of times and I didn't react the right way, or fast enough."

"I hear where you're coming from. But I believe you did what you could."

She swiped the tears from her eyes with the back of her hand.

"You loved him with your whole being. To love someone with all of your heart is the only thing that matters in this world."

She gave a little nod.

He tugged her hands twice. "I imagine there's a lot of turmoil twisting you in knots. Frustration over not knowing, sorrow over his loss and what might have been and the things that never were." He peered into her eyes. "And tinges of loneliness and fear."

Statements, not questions. And he was right. She nodded again. "You get me."

"Cami, honey, I'd like to pray for you, with you."

She shrugged. "I don't think God cares about people like me."

"Oh, He does. He loves each and every one of us." With her hands still in his hold, he bowed his head. She did the same.

"Dear Father, please lift this burden of grief and guilt from your daughter, Cami. May your light and love find its powerful way into Cami and Danny's heart, reminding them always of your unconditional love. Amen."

Powerful words. Good heart. She looked into his eyes.

"God loves you. He loves all of us. You're no different, but just as wonderful."

She smiled. Around Gavin, smiling was becoming easier and easier. "Thank you for the lovely reminder."

They stared at their united hands. She loved how their intertwined fingers helped her to relax. A wave of acceptance spread throughout her, chasing the last bit of turmoil away.

He stroked her inner-wrists. "I think trouble occurs in this world when people lose sight that God intervenes in our lives and carries us forward through otherwise impossible times. We'd be stuck if it weren't for Him."

"Grace, I guess you can say."

"Yes."

Danny ran into the kitchen at full speed.

"Mom, Mom, did you see her?"

"Who?"

"MJ. She went missing when I dropped her cage and the door flew open."

"Ah," Gavin said. "The mystery crash."

Cami stood and placed her hands on her hips. "There's more you need to learn about Danny and me."

He lifted a brow.

"There's never a *mystery* noise in this house." She tousled her son's hair. "Let's go, buddy. Let's find Miss Mary Jane, together."

"Can Gavin help us?"

He already had helped immensely.

"Want to lend another hand?" she asked.

"Thought you'd never ask."

The three trudged into the living room after one pet hamster. Not a bad way to end a tense, sad afternoon. Not bad, at all.

She passed a framed photograph of her, Todd, and Danny. Yes, God loved her. That was mighty powerful stuff. With her spirits lifted, she pushed aside her old way of fretting over how long this sense of peace could last.

And thought about Gavin. Was he thinking about her as he searched for the hamster?

9

*D*anny slurped his morning orange juice then thudded his empty glass onto the kitchen table. "Mom, I don't think it's a hot idea to ask Ethan to join Friends."

Cami tightened her fingers around her coffee mug and flinched from the jabbing pain. "What's wrong? I thought you like Ethan."

Danny shrugged.

Odd. Danny and Ethan had gotten along well at the park. Maybe he needed some personal space. He usually came around to explaining himself in more detail given extra time. Her curiosity got the best of her. She'd try changing the topic right now to see the result.

"Did you feed your hamster this—"

"Gavin thinks Ethan is cool." Danny shuffled the juice glass between his hands. "He thinks everyone is cool."

"That's good."

"No, Mom. You don't get it. Ethan's different from the rest of the boys in school."

His classmate definitely had a far from stellar rep. However, this was the first time her son alluded to his classmate in an unflattering undertone. "Tell me more."

"He's kinda mean."

"No one else is rough in your class?"

"He's worse than rough. It's hard to explain. He does weird things."

"Being different from the rest isn't necessarily grounds for not treating someone nicely."

Danny narrowed his eyes. "I heard you and Dad talk about how you used to do weird stuff to kids because they were different from you." He started to fidget with his curly blue straw, splattering the droplets of juice stored in the straw.

Cami grabbed a napkin and jabbed at the juice drops on the table then crumpled the cloth in her palm. She'd been foolish to cling to the now obvious false notion that she could keep truths from her son.

"Yes, Danny. I went along with several other neighborhood kids against a family we decided was unlike us and treated them badly." Should she explain how the family happened to be the Kinkaids? No not a good idea. At least, not this given moment. She didn't want to influence her son's developing relationship with Gavin. She hoped this thinking wouldn't explode on her. It was bad enough the admission of her collaboration with the kids from her past would surely result in her little honey's respect of her to wobble on a precarious cliff. A total loss of respect from him would spell pure devastation.

She ran her tongue over her dried lips. "We called them names. We made things unpleasant for them. It was wrong, and I'm ashamed and sorry about our behavior. Now that I'm more mature and know right from wrong, I try to be nice to everyone."

"I can't imagine you like that. You do a good job at being nice, Mom."

She shook her head, wishing she could shake free from the

weight of those burdensome years. "I try my best to be." Her tone was soft; she feared unconvincing.

A frown wrinkled his forehead. "You were way different back then."

Here it comes...the judgment from the one person that meant everything to her. And she couldn't blame him.

Danny smiled softly, appearing more contemplative than happy. "But now you're cool."

"And you're my precious son. I love you, jellybean." She pulled him into a hug, unable to push aside how tense he felt. "The Friends program might be perfect for Ethan. We all need companionship. All boys need good role models. Ethan's no exception."

"Like Gavin is for me?"

"Yes." She sipped her coffee.

"Gavin likes both of us."

"He seems to."

"Yeah. But, there's more."

Ever since she could remember, Danny's special sixth sense and unique perception of people always made her think twice. She knew better than to dismiss it as an overactive imagination. "Like what?"

"You don't think it was cool how he helped clean the popcorn mess up from the floor? Or, how he spent time looking for MJ?"

Thankful that they were now off the subject of her past wrongs, her thoughts drifted to yesterday's events. Her meeting Gavin at the DMV. How he reached out to her in comfort and then side by side on the floor when the popcorn spelled. He'd crawled on his hands and knees, searching under the sofa for the hamster. The end result was a true treasure: Danny and she were able to smile again, from both the inside and outside.

Gavin wanted to make amends with her. But she was the one holding out, the one reserved and removed.

Her coffee cold, she pushed aside the mug. "You're right, sweetheart. Gavin is cool. He sure likes being our neighbor."

"You're not following me, Mom."

The phone rang. Tempted to let the voicemail answer the call so she could ask Danny for details, she decided to pick up. It was early on a Saturday morning. She couldn't imagine disastrous news.

"Camille, help me."

"Mother?" Seldom did Theresa Hitchcock phone, let alone ask her or anyone for help. "What's wrong?"

"I've hurt my knee. An ambulance is on the way. Meet me at the hospital. Your father's out of town." Her mother's voice broke. "I have no idea where your sisters are."

"I'll be there right away."

Her mom severed the connection with a loud sigh.

"Terrific."

Danny pushed his glass aside. "What's wrong, Mom?"

"Get your coat. Grandma's hurt. We have to meet her at the hospital right away."

"Can we pray first?"

At times like these, Cami wished her up and down beliefs in God and His love for her were firmer, like a sturdy dock to stand upon over choppy waters.

"Pray on the way, buddy. There's no time to waste."

"But Gavin says praying is always good."

"Please, let's go."

Danny ran for his coat, talking aloud to God. About to walk out the door, he said amen.

"Amen," she echoed, aware of the emptiness within her swirling about painfully. She wanted to have faith in God. Just wasn't sure how to get reacquainted again.

❄

$\mathcal{K}$indred Lake Regional Hospital held distinct memories for Cami. A few pleasant ones. Some not. On a bright, warm May morning she gave birth to a beautiful and healthy son, her Danny. A morning when everything in the world moved in the right direction and at the right time. Her baby boy, her heart. Yet, this same place was where Todd refused a psychological evaluation, and afterwards, the hospital where she had identified his body.

As they walked into the lobby, Danny grasped her hands. "It will be okay."

She smiled. "Thanks, Danny." He sought to give her comfort rather than the other way around. In some respects, he was the stronger of the two of them. He'd make some woman a wonderful husband one day.

"Whoa. Mom, your hands are ice cold."

"With you holding them they'll warm fast. Thanks, partner."

Cami located a waiting area with a TV to distract Danny. She then hurried to the ER admitting desk to inquire about her mother. A staff attendant led her to the fourth bay where a nurse waited for the reading of her mom's blood pressure and temperature.

"Hello, Mother."

Theresa frowned and pointed to the thermometer in her mouth in obvious disgust. The second the nurse removed the instrument she began a litany of complaints. Cami held back a sigh. She got that her mother was uncomfortable and in pain, but as much as she had tried to brace for the protests, all the tight threads holding her together began to unravel and she felt hopelessly like a five-year-old again.

"What kept you, Camille? It's been a half hour or more since I phoned. Don't I count on your priority list?"

"We hurried as best as we could."

"Where's Danny?"

"He's in the waiting area."

"Why are you leaving an eight-year-old alone in a big hospital? You of all people should know how children get into mischief if left unattended."

"Oh, I'm familiar with children just a wee bit." The word *Mother* dangled on Cami's lips. She'd always called her Mother, the more formal term Theresa insisted upon. If only her mom could shower her with love. Cami would give the affection right back.

Wait a second.

She peered at her mother writhing on the ER examination table. That was it. No more dreaming. No more wishing upon a magic star for a whole different life. Today she'd take that first step, just like Danny and she had chatted about.

She patted her mother's hand. "Mom..." She paused when her mother's eyes widened. Had her word choice shaken her that much? She swallowed, determined to go forward. "I'm sorry you're hurting. The doctor will ease your discomfort shortly. Don't trouble yourself over Danny. He'll be fine."

"What doctor? They propped my knee on these pillows, but do you think I saw the doctor yet? Of course not. I have to be bleeding to death or clutching at my heart in order to be seen right away. The irony of it all is that the nurses won't treat my pain until I see the doctor. I will never have another foolish scatter rug again in my house to trip over."

A man in his thirties wearing blue scrubs pulled the bay area's curtain back.

Disapproval stretched across her mom's face. "Finally, a doctor. I hope. You're certainly a young one."

"Mom..."

"I'm Doctor Weldon." He smiled at her mother and winked at Cami. "Feistiness in patients can signal good things, like you're holding your own."

Yes, strength was a good asset to have. Yet, day-by-day, Cami was discovering she needed more. Gavin's dreamy eyes flashed before her. He hadn't lived an easy life but certainly stood on two firm feet. He credited his faith for how he'd made it so far.

She had a lot to think about. Later. Between her earlier half-baked confession to her son and aware she'd have to deal with a full disclosure sooner than later, the guilt over her husband, and her mom in the hospital, the time for straightening out her life seemed as far away as the moon. All this was on top of coming to grips with her growing attraction to Gavin.

"I'll soon have you up and about, Theresa," Dr. Weldon said. He then explained he'd have an orderly transport her to radiology for x-rays.

Cami thanked the doctor who then left. She faced her mom.

"I'll wait with Danny, and phone Dad. As for my busy sisters, I'll track them down and update them about your condition."

"Camille, is my grandson still believing in God these days?"

"He is."

"Ask Danny to say a prayer for his tough, old grandmother."

The cold within Cami warmed. She offered a little smile. "I'll definitely ask Danny to pray for you. I'll do the same."

"You?" Theresa's brows furrowed deeply. "I guess I can use all the help I can get."

Whether her mother appreciated it or not Cami leaned over and kissed her on the forehead. "You're in God's loving hands. You'll be fine. Rest. I'll be right outside." She hurried from the curtained off area before her mom could ask her questions she might not know the answers to. Like, if she believed in God. Like, if she believed He could love even her. She might have said those words to her mom in an effort to comfort her, yet she was the one who wanted His love so badly and needed to know if she was worthy of His love.

In the waiting area, Danny stood. Concern etched his face. "Will Grandma get better?"

Cami nodded then shared with him the details she thought he could understand without upsetting him.

"Is this like when Dad died?"

"Oh, no, Danny." She draped an arm around his shoulders and pulled him to her side. "Grandma hurt her knee. The doctor expects her to make an excellent recovery. She asked whether you would pray for her."

"I will."

"I know, honey. You're great."

"No I'm not. God is great."

She smiled. She could learn a thing or two from her son.

"God is certainly good," came from behind her.

Gavin. She'd recognize that strong voice any time or anywhere.

"I forgot to tell you, Mom," Danny began. "I called Gavin. I thought it would be best if he were here with us. You know, so we don't feel alone."

Oh, how she did know intimately those tender feelings. "Thanks, sweetheart." She looked from Danny to Gavin. "You must be loaded down with studies. I feel badly for pulling you away. We would have been fine just the two of us."

"Ah, Cami. It's all good. I'm glad Danny's comfortable enough with me to call in an emergency. Hospitals can be scary places to hang around in."

No debate there. "Thanks for coming. I appreciate it." And there was one more thing she didn't have to think twice about saying. "You have this way of helping me relax."

"I try." He flashed a warm smile then gestured toward a row of chairs and they sat. "I left the second I got word."

"You must have flown."

"Yeah, on angel's wings." Danny giggled. "That would have been awesome."

Gavin chuckled. "There's a story to catch people's attention."

Danny's brows lowered and he squinted. "Grandma wants me to pray for her. She's never asked that before. I hope she's okay."

"She'll be better than ever soon. The doctor will take good care of her. In the meantime, praying is a great idea." Gavin grasped Cami's hand and gave it a gentle squeeze.

Thankful to have his fortitude to lean on, another wave of relief washed over her. But, there was something more. A sizzling force flowed between them, jumping from his fingers to hers. The connection was as strong as the sun's ray breaking through thick clouds. Hospital or no hospital, she couldn't deny a new liveliness blossoming within her. She trailed her gaze from their laced fingers to his arm and up to his handsome face. She liked what she saw.

"Gavin, can you help me pray?" Danny asked.

"Sure, chief."

They bowed their heads. Gavin thanked God for being with them during both good and troubling times and asked for health and mercy for Theresa.

Cami looked up. "Thank you. Do you mind watching Danny while I call my family?"

"If Danny doesn't mind watching me."

Danny smirked. "You?"

Gavin ribbed Danny in the side. "I might get into trouble."

"But you're an adult. You can't get into trouble."

The two exchanged whispers and laughed.

"You two behave," she said in a pretend-authoritative tone. "I'm stepping outdoors for fresh air and to make calls. I'll be right back."

She glanced over her shoulder to see Gavin slip from his jacket pocket a Tootsie Roll. He offered the treat to Danny. Ah, candy. Sweets from a sweet man, one who was sweet toward her as well.

Sweet and hot looking.

This all spelled trouble. She still hadn't apologized to him directly about her actions all those years ago, even after he'd admitted he'd forgiven her. Considering how bad things were between them when they were children, she should leave well enough alone and push aside this strong attraction toward him, once and for all. She needed to stick to the nice-neighbor role. Look how she'd negatively impacted her own husband's life. She certainly didn't want to hurt Gavin, or anyone, again.

❄

*W*ith Danny in the restroom, Gavin's thoughts raced back to Cami, not that they ever strayed far from her. He couldn't stop thinking about her. Didn't want to. Back in November when he'd first met her as his potential new neighbor, his reserves spiked. He figured he'd do as Jesus commanded and offer the proverbial *other cheek* and do no wrong to her or her son. Her stunning looks and gentle nature shortly, in seemingly seconds, turned his game plan upside down and inside out. Those two traits, combined with Cami's patience, sincerity, and her love for others, demonstrated with loving her son and caring for other children at Little Bears, intensified his attraction like a bee combing a flower in the summertime. A woman now, Cami was quite the opposite of the little bratty girl who went along with the neighborhood bullies. People change. With the foolish animosity between them from their childhood days gone, he was gripped by a new full-throttle wish.

Nope. No wish. It was desire.

Romantic desire.

For Cami. But, he'd been sucker-punched when he'd fallen fast and hard for Ariel and then they'd parted because of lack of sustainable interest on her part. That was when he'd turned his focus onto making a new career. He didn't have time in his life for a relationship, let alone take his chances on love again.

Whoa. Love? As in, fall in love with Cami? A second ago he

thought on the level of desire. He was a normal guy, still in his prime. But love?

He kneaded the bunching muscles on the back of his neck as he recalled his earlier phone conversation with one of his sisters...

"Why are you bothering to associate with *that person*?" Denise had asked.

"She has a name. Cami. And she's no longer the troublemaker girl who used to toss insults like grenades. Besides, I can't help to be involved with her. She's my neighbor. Her son and I are partnered together at a group down at the community center."

"There's an easy fix," Denise said. "Quit the group, put your house back on the market, and move far away from her. Fast."

"Yeah, right." He generally didn't do sarcasm, but he hoped his sis got his gist. "I just moved into this house. I'm not going anywhere."

"How unfortunate. While I don't want you to move from Kindred Lake, I do want you separated from her. Pop feels the same way. I'm sure you don't need a reminder about what that Hitchcock girl and the others did to us."

"Of course not." He sighed. His sister would take him down memory lane whether he wanted to go there or not. "And remember, it's not Hitchcock any longer, but Richardson."

"Whatever. She made life pretty rotten for us. She jeered right along with the others. Truth be told, she probably helped to throw those rocks and bricks at our windows. I'm sure you remember the one that struck me."

He rested his eyes shut then, picturing the time fifteen-year-old Denise ran into the kitchen one summer day, blood spurting from her leg.

"Hey little brother. You're a Kinkaid. And we Kinkaid kids made a vow to Pop."

The *vow*. He couldn't forget the source of several restless nights' sleep. He and his sisters had promised never to forgive

Cami and the other kids. It wasn't the Christian thing to do, but his pop wasn't a believer in God. Gavin had gone along with the plan figuring he never needed to worry about keeping their promise since most of the neighborhood kids left Kindred Lake after high school. The few stragglers kept far from them, busy with their own lives. Besides, he'd gone along with the silly promise to get Pop off his back, once and for all.

Denise's irritated exhale jolted him from his thoughts. "Has Ms. Bully apologized?"

He gripped the phone receiver tight. "She's a widow with a young son—"

"Answer my question, Gavin."

He remained silent.

She groaned into the phone. "I thought so. Listen, single parenthood isn't an exemption from apologizing. Get as far away from her as possible. You'll make Pop happy. He's been a grump since what's her name and her son visited."

He ended the call, telling his sister he had a life to live and it was his alone to choose how. Not his finest moment, but he couldn't wrap his mind around any of his sisters encouraging him to perpetuate a grudge of hatred.

Pop needed to forgive Cami, no way around it. It was time to keep the past in the past...

Gavin looked up from his waiting room seat in time to see Danny walking back from the restroom. Question marks etched his eyes.

He plopped onto his seat. "Did I miss anything?"

"A pony."

The kid scrunched his brows together. "Huh? Is this a joke?"

"I wouldn't joke about a pony."

Danny's eyes widened. "Why was a pony in the hospital?"

"He couldn't sing."

Danny inched forward to the edge of his seat. "Why couldn't the pony sing?"

"Because, he was a little hoarse," Gavin said in his best froggy imitation.

Danny thought for a moment then laughed. "Oh, brother. That was good. Got another?"

He pointed toward the corridor. "I do, but there's your mom." He breathed in deeply, unable to ignore how strong his heart beat, a seemingly constant reaction whenever he saw this gorgeous woman.

"Hi, guys."

"Mom, Gavin just told a funny joke." He repeated it for his mom.

Her smile faded to slightly parted lips. Her brows lifted.

"You okay, Cami?" he asked.

"Just frazzled." She sank to the seat beside her son. "I reached one sister, who will call the other. Left a message for my father at his hotel." She glanced around. "Guess we're still waiting to hear from the doctor?"

"It's taking forever," Danny mumbled. His attention drifted to a game show playing on the television bolted to the wall.

Gavin sat silently with Cami. In the back of his mind his sister's voice resounded like a scratchy CD of a lousy song. *You're a Kinkaid. And we Kinkaid kids made Pop a vow.* But this wasn't the time or place to bring up a foolish promise. Cami had enough on her mind with her mom under doctor's care. Yet, he couldn't rest unless he could help her relax.

"Hey, there," he whispered, not wanting to catch Danny's attention. "You're rightly concerned about your mom's health, but I can tell something else is also troubling you."

She smoothed a wrinkle in her jeans. "Is it obvious?"

He nodded.

"It's a difficult time. My mother and I don't have the greatest of relationships. Never did. Times like this make the strain heavier."

"I can understand how it's a bit uncomfortable to see her

hurting."

"That's putting it mildly. We have one of those surface mother-daughter relationships. You know, Happy Mother's Day. Happy Birthday. How's my grandson, Camille? We've been like that forever. I should be used to it, but I'm not." She hugged her middle. "I'll level with you, Gavin. Seeing her in pain and dependent upon me renews my grief and longing for a close relationship, one which we never had. I've been made aware—again—how a closer bond is a key missing ingredient in my life. In both of our lives."

"Life's not over."

"My coping abilities are shot right now."

He grasped her hand. "If you'd like, I'll accompany you to see her when the time comes."

"I would appreciate that, if I'm not wearing your patience thin. Danny and I are leaning a lot on you lately."

"Good." He squared his shoulders back. "I have pretty big shoulders and they're yours for leaning on."

She smiled. "Thanks."

"That's what neighbors and friends are about."

"Friends," she repeated.

"Ms. Richardson?"

Cami stood to greet Dr. Weldon. "How's Mom?"

The doctor eyed Gavin and Danny. "Would you like to step aside into a private corner, Ms. Richardson?"

"Right here's fine."

"You mom's knee is bruised pretty badly, but nothing more serious. No surgery necessary. However, her blood pressure is sky high. I'd like to keep her overnight to treat and monitor her condition."

"Wow." Cami grasped the collar of her blouse. "It's a shame Mom hurt herself, but considering she hates going for a physical, she's fortunate enough you've discovered this hidden problem before a more serious one occurred."

"Yes. I believe we caught this in time before your mom experienced complications."

At her side, Gavin murmured praise to God. He slipped his hand around Cami's.

"We'll settle her in a room and then you can visit. You probably have an hour on your hands if you'd like to catch a breath of air."

Cami thanked the doctor. After he left she faced Danny and Gavin. "I need a cup of coffee. Anyone else hungry or in need of a drink?"

"I want a snack," Danny said, a little on the loud side. He cupped his hand over his mouth.

Gavin patted the boy's shoulder. "I'd love a cup of coffee."

"Okay, then. I'll alert a nurse we'll be gone for just a short time." Cami glanced at the floor then right back at him. "My mother could be a handful at times."

"Relax. My charm and good looks will transform her."

Her cheeks colored a soft pink. "I like your self-confidence but sorry to say, I doubt it when it comes to Theresa Hitchcock. She's not the type of person who readily changes."

"We can trust God, Mom," Danny said.

"Spoken like a true believer," Gavin said. Danny's gentle reminder came at a perfect time. Doubts had clouded his mind. Worries too. Would Cami see him as impulsive? He didn't want to cause trouble. Surely, her mother wouldn't recognize his name. He sighed to himself. Like Danny said, trust in God.

They rode the elevator to the downstairs cafeteria. Danny ordered a Caesar salad; he and Cami stuck to coffee.

An hour later, to the minute, while Danny remained in the fourth floor's waiting room, Gavin and Cami slipped into her mother's room. She had been asleep, but started to stir. They moved beside her bed.

"Hello, Mom," Cami said.

Aware of her trepidation, Gavin admired Cami's caring tone.

Theresa blinked several times. "Oh, I must have drifted off."

"How are you?"

"Like I'm on a sinking cruise ship and didn't get to sample those fancy banquets." She started to cough. Cami reached out to her, but her mom waved her off.

"I'm concerned about you. The doctor says it's a good thing he caught your high blood pressure when he did." She trailed a finger along the bedrail. "I want you around for a long time to come. I love you, Mom."

Gavin smiled at Cami. He didn't know many adults who could openly talk about their love for each other, let alone to an estranged parent.

"Who's that?"

Cami worried her lips. "Mom, this is Gavin. He waited with Danny and me for the doctor and then led us in prayer for your health."

"Oh." She narrowed her eyes. "What's your last name?"

"Mom..."

He leaned over the bedrail. "I'm an old childhood acquaintance, Gavin Kinkaid."

"I must be more exhausted then I thought and not hearing correctly. Did you say Kinkaid?"

Cami's breath hitched audibly. Gavin hated to add stress, but he wasn't ashamed of himself or his family.

"Yes, Mrs. Hitchcock. I'm Gavin Kinkaid. I went to school with Cami."

Theresa faced Cami. "Get him away from me."

"We just prayed for you and—"

"I don't care. Make him leave." She coughed again and pressed the nurse's page button resting on her lap.

Gavin squeezed Cami's shoulder. "I'll wait outside with Danny."

He left the room before she could object.

10

"*N*ext time, Camille, don't do me favors by bringing *him* here. I don't need visitors like him slowing down my recovery."

Cami's temples pounded. "I don't understand..." Her heart ached to again call her mother *Mom*, but her tongue spiked with the sour taste and tease of the more formal Mother. If only her mom would open the door of love and warmth, Cami would jump right in without a blink of an eye. For now, she'd deal with the choices of endearments later, when things calmed down. "The Kinkaids never harmed any one of us. Let's face the truth. I was the one who caused the trouble. But Gavin lifted you in prayer for returned health. That must ring pretty wonderful to have someone caring enough to pray for your recovery."

"If you'd like me to get well, please don't disturb me about someone who doesn't deserve my attention."

Cami's mouth dropped open. It took a few seconds to push words out. In a world where people often neglected to give two heartbeats for each other, her mother should have rejoiced in Gavin's care and concern for her. "I don't get this thing about Gavin not *deserving* your attention? He's never wronged you."

"Evidently, he's never done anything right either." She fixed one of her mother-stares at her. "I don't recall you going out of your way to pal-up with this...this..."

"This man. Gavin is a man, like any other, and should have your respect."

"He's a Kinkaid. What's the difference now, Camille?"

She was slammed back into her childhood days. *Little girls don't question their mothers. What I say, Camille, goes. Never forget we're a good family, but remember there are less suitable people from objectionable households and that is the bottom line around here.*

Cami had then stamped her foot, acting like the petulant child she didn't want to be, and not at all like the mature twelve-year-old, nearly a teenager, she was. "Isn't that prejudice," she'd shouted at her mother. "Isn't that plain nasty?"

She was sent to her room.

When repetitive attempts of changing her parents' attitudes and perception failed, on top of peer pressure later from the cool kids in high school, she followed along. Whether her taunts against the Kinkaid family were right or wrong no longer mattered. Not wanting to risk alienation from her family, she shoved her fading morals into a dust-covered file in her mind. With her beloved great-aunt Fran's passing, all she had in the big wide world were her mother, father, and two sisters. No way would she dare forfeit the only people that cared for her.

Until she became an adult and moved on with her life.

Until she had a child of her own and swore to herself she'd do whatever it took to make sure her precious boy didn't dish out or suffer from social hatred.

Now, looking at her mother squirming about in a hospital bed because she battled high blood pressure, how could she respond without aggravating her more? Words failed to come. She glanced upward, desperate. *God, what should I do? Please help me.*

The immediate answer rocked her back on her heels.

Love your mom.

Really? Cami grimaced, mentally apologizing to God. Who was she to question Him?

"I love you, Mom. Tell me, what can I do to make you more comfortable?"

The nurse's call button slid from her hand. "I...uh, oh...I'm tired."

Cami leaned over the bedrail. "Of course you are. Your condition has taken its toll."

"I've suffered no such toll. I knew what I was saying when what's his name was here."

"You relax."

"Where's the nurse I called for?"

"I'm right here," a reddish-haired fiftyish woman said as she walked into the room. "And I'm going to check your vitals then see to it you're nice and relaxed. Under my charge, my patients are happy and comfortable ones."

Cami chuckled to herself. Her mom might have just met her match.

The nurse recorded the blood pressure and heart monitor reading then smiled warmly. "My name's Lorraine, and you can always call me whenever you need to, sweetie. What was all the commotion about? We heard you down at the nurse's station. Are you're in pain?"

"I sure am."

"On a scale of one to ten, with ten being the worst pain, please rate your pain for me."

"It flew off the chart when that man stood before me."

"Do you mean the handsome guy who just left your room?" Lorraine wiped her brow with an exaggerated swipe of her hand. "We nurses were planning to draw coffee stirrers to see who'd get to detain that piece of eye candy a wee longer with a dozen or more questions."

Cami glanced out the window to conceal both a joyous grin and a burning flush heating her cheeks. Gavin definitely pleased the eyes. Her eyes.

"How does your pain rate?" Lorraine pressed.

"About four, I guess. I'm more sleepy than anything else."

"Good. We like sleepy patients. A little snooze will do wonders."

Cami turned in time to catch the nurse's wink.

"I'll try to sleep," Theresa said, struggling to keep her eyes open.

"You've been through a lot. You need a little shuteye to recoup your energy."

"Sounds good," Theresa agreed.

"Maybe then," Lorraine continued, "you won't be tossing out visitors. Especially, someone in the tall and good-looking department like the nice-looking gentleman we were just chatting about. Visitors are precious—we have patients without family or friends. Hospitals can be a lonely place."

Cami nodded in agreement before she could wonder if her mom had noticed. But really, it didn't matter. She was a grown woman. As a child she'd made wrong choices. As an adult, she knew better and could make wiser ones. It was time to let go of the past, which no longer defined her. And that also meant her mother's opinions of her.

"Good-looking..." Theresa murmured.

"And she's off to slumber-land," Lorraine said to Cami. "You can breathe."

Not realizing she'd been holding her breath, Cami exhaled. "Guess I'm pretty tense, after all. I've always had trouble dealing with my mom's strong ways."

Lorraine fingered the cross she wore around her neck. She smiled gently. "Honey, I can't say I blame you. A forceful personality can be unsettling to others. Yet, toughness can also be a virtue. It can help one in places where otherwise it's rough, like recovering in a hospital."

"True."

"Sometimes, that trait is a cover-up for fear. Of people, places, possibilities, or one's own vulnerabilities."

"For fear..." Cami mused. Lorraine had a good grasp on her mother.

"If you ask me, we're put in situations where we're not comfortable, and with people who can be stressful, for interesting reasons. Not that I've figured out why." The pager, fastened to Lorraine's shirt pocket, buzzed. "Ah, a nurse's job is never done. I hope God has a new pair of feet for me this Christmas." She headed toward the door.

"Wait. I'd like to thank you."

The nurse was gone, perhaps onto her next patient. Cami would inquire about a way to thank the woman for her kindness.

She grasped the bedrail tight. Again, she glanced upward. "Thanks, God." Rusty, she tried praying for her mother's recovery and for the end of hostilities between her family and the Kinkaids. After amen, she started for the door. Her immediate concern was to find Danny. And, of course, Gavin. Definitely, Gavin.

Inches to the door, she stopped short. This was the first time she had actually prayed for the end of wrongdoings against the Kinkaid family. Changes. They were happening.

The nurse's words drifted through her mind. *We're put in situations...for interesting reasons.* She needed to figure out why she was in this particular situation and if God had planted her there for a reason. Surely meeting Gavin after years of separation was no mere coincidence.

"Mom," Danny called from the doorway.

"Danny? I'd asked you to stay in the waiting area down the hall."

"What's happening? Gavin didn't look happy when he rushed past me."

"Grandma will be fine. She's sleeping." Her son's words

crashed into her overcrowded thoughts. "Where's Gavin? He said he'd wait with you."

"At first, he did. Then he said he needed air and went outside."

What-ifs flooded her mind. What if Gavin didn't want to bother with them a minute longer? What if he planned to confront her mom about her choice of words? What if... Cami gulped. What if he put his house up for sale?

She guided Danny toward the elevator. No. She would not participate in the dreadful what-if game her imagination taunted her with. Gavin would be waiting for her. She needed to trust in God.

"I don't see him anywhere," Danny said when they stepped outdoors.

A scan across the parking lot didn't reveal his car.

He was gone.

11

Don't answer it. Gavin grimaced at his cell phone on the passenger seat as if an unruly rider had just barked out a slew of obscenities. His heart twisted.

Let it go, and no one gets hurt.

No way. That was the lame way of doing things. Always striving to be compassionate, he wasn't about to venture into insensitivity by ignoring a phone call, especially since he knew it was Cami. An arrow of alarm coiled his neck muscles. Her mom might have taken a turn for the worse. Or, was something up with Danny?

Voicemail picked up the call. He pulled off the county road and punched in her number.

She answered right away. "Hi, Gavin. So glad I caught you."

All he could see in his mind's eye were her beautiful lips spread in a sunny smile. Hopefully, upon hearing his voice, they'd stay smiling. He suppressed a groan. He'd just bailed on her and here he was imagining her stuck on him and wishing him back. While he couldn't stop thinking about her, he wouldn't blame her if she wanted to never see him again.

"I shouldn't have left," he said.

"After the way my mother treated you, I can't blame you."

"It was wrong of me. Sorry."

"Sorry?"

"Yes."

"Most men I know don't apologize."

"Cami, I've never been like most men."

She chuckled, music in his ear. Seconds flicked by and she asked his whereabouts.

"About two miles down the road, sitting on the shoulder, thankful you answered the call."

"Thankful," she echoed, puffing an appealing mix of brightness and surprise into his ear.

"How's your mom?"

"Sound asleep. A nurse came in and calmed her right down. She'll be fine."

"Mom," Danny said in the background. "I'm hungry."

"Again?"

Never slow when it came to maximizing a situation for the positive, he jumped in. "Want to meet me at the diner where I bumped into you and Danny, the place that served those amazing pancakes?"

"You've been away from Kindred Lake too long. Rick's the only diner in town."

"I can be there in ten minutes."

"Sounds great."

He said goodbye, disconnected the call, and stared at the phone. Yep. Meeting Cami did sound great. He better not blow it this time.

*C*ami, sitting beside her son, eyed his plate. Surely, his untouched hamburger and fries had duplicated right before her eyes. "You're not hungry?"

Danny dropped his gaze to his dish. "Just thinking about Grandma. She was so upset."

Cami put her arm around Danny and pulled him closer. She peeked at Gavin.

"Tell him," he mouthed.

Before she could attempt a response, Jacey, the waitress who had served them last time, arrived back quickly with a tray of a full coffee carafe and another mug of hot chocolate. "You know these small towns and how fast word gets around, Cami. I just heard about your mom. I hope she's feeling better."

"She'll be fine. My two sisters should be flying in tonight—if they can catch a flight. They're trying to contact our dad."

The frizzy-blond waitress smiled, and topped off their coffee mugs and placed before Danny his second cocoa. Cami usually didn't allow him to indulge in too many sweets, but an injured grandmother and his subsequent concern ranked up there for a little comforting.

"Nothing like an emergency to bring on a family reunion, of sorts," Jacey said. She glanced at Gavin then back at Cami. "You two want any lunch or just sticking to coffee."

"I'm fine," Cami said. Gavin echoed.

"Well, I'll be out in a few to see if anyone wants desserts." The young woman buzzed to the next table, order pad in hand.

"Right," Cami muttered. "One big happy reunion."

Gavin reached across the table for her hands. His touch a balm, she relaxed. Danny patted her shoulder.

"You guys are sweet. Just what I need right now." She smiled. "I'm thankful you're both with me."

"Can't imagine it any other way," Gavin said.

And that was the thing. She didn't want it any other way. She felt grounded, appreciated, and comfortable around Gavin. The latter state—*comfortable*—she'd never expected to experience again, with him or any guy. What more, this growing companionship between she, her son, and this special heart-catching man was beginning to replace her emptiness with a snatch of joy. Call her greedy, but the thing was, she wanted a copious amount more of happiness, for not only herself but also her son.

"So, what about Grandma?" Danny slurped his cocoa then set the mug down. "I got bored in the waiting area and headed to her room. Sorry, Mom, that I listened but I couldn't help it. She said mean things about Gavin. Why?"

There was no dodging her son. It was time to level with Danny about what once occurred between her, Gavin, and the other children. He'd have to understand and see through the nonsense, desiring not to repeat it himself. She could only pray he would, and that one day Danny would sit down with his own young children and discourage them about social prejudice.

"Danny, your Grandma raised her voice at Gavin because she's convinced she doesn't like him."

Danny's eyes widened. "That's not right. It's not like they know each other super well."

"It's certainly not right." Cami looked at Gavin. Finished with his coffee, he leaned back into the booth, studying them. No malice filled his eyes. Only encouragement with a hint of curiosity.

She inched closer to Danny. "Remember when we had hot chocolate and cake at Mrs. Kinkaid's the day we went to the library?"

Danny nodded.

"And when you asked if she attends church, do you remember what she said?"

"That it was hard to believe in God when their kids came home crying because other kids made fun of them."

Cami patted his hand. "And why did those children make fun of the Kinkaid kids?"

"Because they didn't live in a nice house like the others did." He shifted his gaze to Gavin then back to her. "Wait. You once told me that you did bad things to some kids. Were you part of those kids who picked on Gavin and his family?"

She swiped at tears streaking down her cheeks. "Yes, Danny. A long time ago when I was a girl I was part of a neighborhood group who bullied Gavin and his family."

"You were a bully, Mom? Why?" He tilted his head. "Gavin, did you do something bad to my mom?"

"No, chief."

Danny rested his palms against the edge of the table and pushed back. "But she's my mom. My mom's a great mom. She wouldn't do anything bad. You must have made this up to get her in trouble."

"Sweetheart," Cami said gently. "Gavin is telling the truth. He was a nice boy then, just like he's a nice man now. Us kids treated him poorly because his house was not fancy like ours, because his dad was an auto mechanic unlike our fathers who worked in offices and wore suits and shiny dress shoes. These were all silly reasons. Our parents also said nasty things about the Kinkaids and we copied them without asking them to explain themselves. We were wrong." She dropped her gaze. "I'm ashamed of my behavior."

"Didn't you know better, Mom? You don't do things like that now. How come you didn't stop the other kids?" Danny fiddled with his spoon. "I still don't get Grandma. Mrs. Kinkaid invited us in for cake. She was awesome. And Gavin's super nice to us, and fun to be with. But Grandma acted like Gavin and his family are bad."

The waitress arrived back with a look of hope in her eyes and dessert menus in hand. After a quick look around the table she murmured she'd be back in a few minutes. Cami mouthed *thank-you*, but Jacey had moved away fast to respect their privacy. If only Cami had learned the value of respect and consideration at a younger age.

"Danny, I wanted the other kids to like me and that's why I

acted just like them. That meant that I wasn't nice to all of my neighbors."

"That's the opposite of what you teach me. And what God says not to do."

Danny understood. He also remembered his Sunday school lessons well, considering he hadn't attended for a few years.

"Correct."

Danny looked directly into Gavin's eyes. "You must be upset with Mom."

"No, I'm not. I forgive her, and the others."

"I'm sorry." Cami clasped Gavin's hands. "I was wrong to put you and your family through so much suffering. I should have apologized years ago."

He gave a little nod. "Apology accepted. Gratefully."

Sincerity and kindness sparkled in his eyes, making him more handsome than ever. She leaned toward him, wanting to touch him, wanting to be touched by him. Danny chinked his cup against his dish. She jumped back against her chair.

"I still don't get why Grandma is mean to Gavin. Why isn't she nice like you?"

Ah, the million dollar question. Cami wished her mother would soften her ways and become more loving and gentle. About to tell Danny of her lack of understanding when it came to her own mother, Gavin held up a hand.

"Cami, I'd like to try explaining."

Appreciating his confident tone, she nodded. She surprised herself by reaching for one of Danny's fries, hungry, after all.

"Danny," Gavin begun, "it's like that story I began telling when I watched you the afternoon you were sick."

"I kind of remember. I think I fell asleep. The story about ice cream?"

"Good memory, chief."

Cami couldn't imagine where Gavin was heading with this one.

"If you recall, the story's about grouchy ice cream factory owners."

"Yep. Why were they grouchy?"

"Beats me. I can't see why they'd complain and fret. They lived in nice houses, enjoyed good health, and loved their wives and children. Little things bothered them though, like spilled coffee, little time to read the comics, or what have you."

Danny bit into his burger. Meat juice drizzled into his dish, and he moved his stack of fries away to keep them dry. "What were their problems?"

Gavin exaggeratedly scratched his head. "None I could see. They had lots to be thankful for, yet they sure weren't happy. They didn't like it when others were happy either."

Danny scrunched up his forehead. "Maybe they ate all the maple-walnut ice cream in the world and froze their brains."

Oh, boy. He wasn't taking this seriously. "Don't be silly, hon."

Gavin waggled a finger. "Actually, Cami, I think Danny's onto something."

She blinked. "Go on. You have me curious."

"You see, these folks ate maple-walnut ice cream every single day. They were crazy for one particular flavor and ate it for breakfast, lunch, and dinner, refusing to try a different kind. Pretty soon, only *their* choice of ice cream and way of life was right. Everyone else was wrong."

"I think I understand. It's like Grandma has been eating maple-walnut ice cream all her life 'cause her parents did, and her grandparents did, and their grandparents did. And no one thought to try another flavor."

Gavin fingered an okay sign. "Absolutely."

Cami rubbed Danny's back. "You're pretty wonderful in the smarts department."

"So, if I eat chocolate ice cream, I'm wrong. If Gavin eats strawberry, he's wrong. And, if you eat vanilla, you're wrong."

"Afraid you're right, chief."

"Danny," Cami said. "We need to come up with a solution to make things right."

Danny stared at his paper placemat. "We can pray. God can help us."

Cami smiled. "Definitely. Do you have any other ideas?"

"Kind of," Danny said without a blink of his eye. "But you said this already. We can hug Grandma 'cause she probably hasn't been hugged enough."

Cami flooded with warmth and pride for her son...and for Gavin. Without his encouragement, this exchange of ideas, let alone her confession to her son, wouldn't have occurred. At least, not at this crucial time.

Oh yes, God was working His wonders.

"Hugging is good," she whispered, too emotional to test the strength of her voice.

Gavin squeezed her hand again. Their gazes locked.

Jacey darted back. "Are those the smiles of dessert expectations?"

"Yes," Cami said. "How about a slice of chocolate pudding pie for each of us, with lots of whipped cream?"

Both Gavin and Danny rubbed their bellies. They looked at each other and then exploded in laughter.

"You got it," Jacey said. "That's my Caleb's favorite. I'll be right back."

Gavin flashed a smile. "I have a suggestion."

"Your eyes are radiating with hope," Cami said. "Tell us."

"We can do more. Let's give this town something to really talk about."

She leaned into the table. "I'm listening."

"We should be seen more often in public, and in a whole different way. Let those who once saw us as enemies now see us as the best of friends."

She leaned against the table, her fingers digging into her forearms. There was that *friends* things again, as in *only* friends. She resisted slumping her shoulders despite the sobering mood over-coming her. This was no time to worry about what kind of ties she had with Gavin. And really, she didn't have any business thinking about a deeper relationship. He had never made a move toward a more intimate level between them. Nor had she. Yet, her insides were tight and twisty feeling, like the fabric of her being was stitched together all wrong.

"Sounds pleasant. Friendship is a great lesson to teach."

"Friendship is a great thing to have between people, especially us two who once never dreamed of it." He looked hard into her eyes. "Are you up to this? The flip side is considering the way our families react to each other, there might be consequences."

"Yes, and that's exactly why I like your suggestion. I'm hoping for consequences—nice ones. And coupled with Danny's brilliant idea to pray and to hug my mom, I believe we have more to gain than to lose."

"I agree, Cami. Let's show our families and community the world will not end because we're friends."

She forced a smile. "Let's go for it."

"If it doesn't interfere with you visiting your mother, let's attend church together, beginning tomorrow. Great place and time."

Danny beamed. "Can we Mom?"

Cami couldn't deny the enthusiasm in her son's voice, nor close her eyes to the ring of promise encircling her rusty heart. It would be their first visit to church since Todd's death.

She peered at Gavin then her son. "Yes. I'd like to attend church, with you."

12

_C_ ami glanced at the mantle clock, likely the tenth time within the past five minutes. She sighed. Everything was in its place, and ready, except for Danny. She tamped down on her patience, determined not to pester her little guy, especially since they weren't late. Yet.

She ran through her checklist again, beginning with her purse. Tissues. Check. Gum for Danny, post-church. Yes. Offering check. Yes. Hurrying from room to room, she did a house check. Coffee maker, unplugged? Yep. Miss Mary Jane, the infamous hamster, tucked happily in her cage? Yes, indeed. Thermostat definitely turned down.

Footsteps rumbled above. Danny would be downstairs any second. She looked into the mahogany-framed mirror by the door. She needed to remember where she'd placed her smile.

What was wrong with her? Yes, she did want to attend church. She loved Danny's bubbling excitement about going to public worship. He believed in God ever since he was old enough to utter the word _God_. And, she had too. _Had_. Past tense, though swinging around for a thankful comeback. Her faith had been tucked away for a while. Gavin had helped her to refocus on the

One who mattered the most. In the mirror's reflection, she caught the corners of her mouth turning upward in a warm smile.

If she could keep that smile in place, she'd be set. There was no reason to be nervous. As Gavin had reminded her when they exited the diner yesterday, God would be happy to see her again in church. He would find a way to make these shaky first steps back easier.

"Wow." Danny jumped off the third step. "You smell nice."

"It's a little dab of perfume. Too strong?"

"Nah. It's pretty. Smells like flowers."

"Roses."

"You've been wearing that stuff a lot lately, like since Gavin moved across the way."

She fussed with her collar. "I like it, that's all."

"Wait until Gavin smells you. He'd like it, too. He'll also like your skirt and blouse."

"Beats penguin and reindeer duds," she mumbled then swallowed hard. She wasn't trying to lure Gavin's—or anyone's—attention. Or was she?

"Mom," Danny said, watching out the window. "He's coming over."

Reality clobbered her and she jumped. She needed to accept the truth. She couldn't fool herself anymore. Gavin was extraordinarily handsome, gentle, and caring. He loved children. Adored Danny. She could no longer deny her attraction to him.

Yep, she was attracted to a man who only wanted her friendship.

Her heartbeat slowed.

All things considering, she couldn't—shouldn't—expect more after all those years of trouble she had caused him.

The doorbell rang.

"I'll get it." Danny rocketed toward the door.

Gavin stepped in, the morning's sunlight announcing him like a prince out of a fairytale.

Her insides fluttered.

She had a problem. A serious one.

"Hey, chief. You're looking sharp."

"Mom said no jeans or T-shirts to church."

"Brown chinos, white shirt, and brown tie are good choices on you." Gavin's gaze leaped to Cami. "And your mom looks amazing."

"And she smells good," Danny added.

"Hmm. Roses." Gavin flashed her a wide grin. "That she does."

The longer he stared, the more she wanted him to.

Danny stepped between them and waved, casting an odd look.

A sheepish expression crossed Gavin's face. "Ready?"

"Yes, we are." Cami turned. "I'll just get my coat and..."

Too late. He'd fetched her coat from the back of the oak rocking chair and held it out for her to slip into.

"Thanks." She slid her arm into a sleeve, bringing her closer to him by mere inches.

He bent close to her neck, inhaled deeply. "Rose is definitely your scent."

And his scent fitted him perfectly. The fresh outdoors twirled with woodsmoke and baked goods, a mix of nature and hearth. Yet, he didn't wear cologne. Just him. And if she stood there a second more, she'd likely embarrass her son by throwing herself at the man...who wanted to be friends. Only. His suggestion. And she'd gone along with it.

She turned away before she couldn't. "Ready, Danny?"

Danny shrugged into his jacket. "Yep."

Gavin held the door open for her. "You look lovely today, Cami. Actually, everyday."

"Yeah, she does," Danny said.

The two guys chuckled in harmony, a lovely sound Cami couldn't deny despite her heart wanting more and her mind reminding her that Gavin was off-limits when it came to the next level of a relationship.

*T*hey arrived at the church a few minutes past the start of the service. As soon as Cami stepped into the small historic stone church with its beautiful glass stained windows, she recognized Pastor Pembroke asking everyone to praise the Lord and to give thanks to Him.

The pastor spread his hands in a gesture that took in the whole congregation. "I see a few familiar faces I haven't seen in a while. Please, feel welcomed. If you derive only one lesson today from my rambling on..." A soft murmur of affectionate chuckles stopped the pastor for a moment. "Know that God loves you, and wants to forgive you of any wrongdoings. The Lord is great, is almighty, and doesn't want to cast you away as an unloved, forgotten child. He is your Father. He wants you in His heart, always."

Gavin slipped his firm but gentle hand around hers. She locked onto his striking grayish-blue eyes. Her spirits lifted. Joy enveloped her like a hug.

At the conclusion of the service, Pastor Pembroke invited everyone into the parish hall for coffee hour.

Danny shot to his feet. "I want to check out the cookies."

About to ask Gavin if he'd like to stay for refreshments, Cami did a double take when Danny seemingly vanished.

Gavin pointed. "Over there."

She spied her son heading toward the church's side door that led to the social hall. She chuckled. "That child of mine can never pass an offer for a good donut or cookie."

"That's one more thing I have in common with Danny."

"Make that chocolate and I can relate."

Gavin helped her out of the pew. He set his hand on her lower back and began to guide her into the thinning crowd. An unfamiliar, yet comforting touch.

Bubbles of excitement raced through her veins. A few rows up, she reached for his hand and pulled him around to face her. "Have a sec before you replenish your sugar supply?"

Without blinking, he replied, "For you, Cami, always. What's up?"

She leaned against the side of the pew before them, running her fingertips across the intricately carved walnut top. Gavin stood before her waiting for her reply, patiently and eagerly. Two qualities in a man she was unaccustomed to. His brows arched in curiosity.

"Without a doubt, I know God has led me back into this church today. And, without a doubt, He spoke to me. Me!" To her own ears she sounded childlike innocent, but she imagined when it came to her faith, that was what He would smile over. "I'm feeling more at ease, and that includes my angst about the past, with you as well as with my husband. Like you've said, I need to accept Todd was a troubled soul. I was a good wife, the best I could be. And I loved him with all my heart." She dropped her gaze.

Gently, he lifted her chin and peered into her eyes. "You're a good person."

"As long as God thinks so...and you."

"And me?"

She nodded.

He leaned toward her, his mouth so close to hers that she couldn't focus on anything else but his sweet lips. Then, he pulled back. "Let's check out the refreshments before a certain eight-year-old snatches them all for himself."

"I like how you think," she said, her voice faltering, stuck on a kiss that didn't happen but one she wanted so badly. Wrong place, wrong time, for sure. This was a house of worship. Then again, they'd agreed to appear in public, together, yet on a platonic level to show this childhood town of theirs that yes, indeed, two former enemies could easily be friends.

He pulled at his chin.

"What?"

He flashed a boyish grin. "I'm getting addicted to being with you."

Her balance became wobbly and she slid into a nearby pew. She hoped she wouldn't utter words she shouldn't.

He reached for her shoulder, his touch setting off an odd mix of sparks and peace. The tranquility was like the needed calm after a storm. But the spark she felt? Undeniably, the electric current of physical attraction.

She had to stop thinking like this. He was a nice guy, a good neighbor. They'd agreed to show others they were friends and friendship was a true gift these days. Nothing more.

"Cami, I didn't bring you here because I see you as someone in need of help."

Her eyes misted. "I wasn't thinking along those lines, but I'm glad to hear that."

"Mom? Gavin?" Danny called from the doorway. "The cookies are almost gone. Don't you want some?"

"You bet I do." Gavin glanced at Cami. "Care to join us?"

"Of course. I can't resist two handsome men." Her words were meant more out of charm and politeness. She hooked arms with him. Delight shined in his eyes. Oh, those handsome lake-blue eyes! Together they walked toward Danny and the crowd on the other side of the door.

*A*s Gavin escorted Cami into the church social hall he couldn't deny his feelings a second longer. Whenever he was with her or thinking about her, his world brightened. His energy soared. He'd daydreamed more than once about sailing into the future with this amazing woman just to see what would happen because he didn't expect anything short of awesome.

But, did it matter? They were friends. They'd agreed upon it. Nothing more.

Decision made. He'd stick to the game plan between them. Together they'd show others how two people who were supposedly on the wrong side of the proverbial tracks could be the best of friends.

Cami pointed across the church hall. "Look, Danny. There's your pal Ethan with his family. Go say hello."

"I don't want to."

"Well, I'm saying hello to Ethan and his folks. Won't you join me?" She put a hand on Danny's shoulder. "They've been under a lot of stress lately. They need supportive friends."

Danny visibly stiffened and dropped his cookie onto the floor. It broke in half, chocolate chips and oatmeal scattered about. "I gotta find the boy's room."

Concern washed over Cami's face as she watched her son duck away. Forget playing it safe. She needed encouragement. Gavin narrowed the distance between them. The instant heat they shared chased away the cold dampness of the social hall. He hoped her spirits warmed too.

"Wonder what that was about?" she said, quietly. "He started to act funny about Ethan yesterday morning."

"I haven't noticed any change in his behavior at Friends."

"I'll try talking with Danny later." She glanced again at Ethan. "Speaking of Friends, I wonder if Ethan will be attending."

"One way to find out."

"Yep. It's been a long time since I've said hi to Ethan's dad, Steve, and that was back in those rotten school days when we caused all that trouble for your family." She grabbed a napkin from the nearby refreshment table and picked up the cookie crumbs from the floor. Before she could spring upright, he bent over and placed his hand on hers.

"It's all right now," he murmured into her ear. "Now is all that counts."

They stood together, locked gazes and nodded. Something more jumped between them. Understanding, support, acceptance. No doubt about it. These tender acts of caring were as palpable as the air around them, necessary for living.

Together, they disposed the cookie pieces into a trash receptacle and headed toward the Mathers family. Janet, Ethan's mother, cordially greeted them. Steve excused himself, saying he needed to check the car. Ethan followed. The younger son remained with his mom.

"My little one seems to be on the track to improved health," Janet said, keeping her eye on her husband and son as they blazed out of the room.

"Wonderful." Cami hooked arms with Gavin.

Her touch fired up Gavin's five senses, making him more than the Gavin Kinkaid who used to watch everyone else enjoy life but never got a handle on it himself. Wait one awful second. He glanced down at their connected arms. This wasn't real. They'd agreed to put on a show of friendship to stir folks socially. *Let's give them something to really talk about.* Him and his big mouth.

"Janet," Cami continued. "This is Gavin Kinkaid. He's a neighbor and friend who is active at the Friends group that meets at the community center."

Janet pulled her little boy closer to her side. "Ah, yes. I'm familiar with the group."

Gavin rushed to chase away the awkwardness. "I enjoy helping others. It's worth volunteering to see a smile return to a child's face. Ethan would enjoy the program."

"We'll have to see what my husband says." Janet glanced at the door exiting to the parking lot. "Speaking of, I better go check on Steve and Ethan."

"Have a lovely day," Cami said.

Janet tilted her head. "You too." She rushed away with her younger son right beside her.

Cami's brows furrowed. "Odd. Something's up."

Without thinking twice, Gavin pulled her tight to his side. "I'd say."

13

*C*ami slipped the car into park on her mom's driveway. "I'll be right around to help you."

"I'm no child, Camille. I can manage myself."

Cami resisted reacting to her mom's antagonistic tone. She waited with ready ears in case her assistance was needed, after all.

Her mom pushed the passenger door open, swung her right leg out, and collapsed back against her seat. A groan escaped her lips. "Spare me an I-told-you-so. Yes, I confess, my knee still hurts."

"Dizzy too?"

She grunted.

"I'll come around." Relieved to help, Cami smiled. "The doctor says you'll be fine again in no time."

Her mother cast a long look. "I hope so."

Cami rushed to the passenger side. The last thing she needed was for her light-headed mom to fall and break a hip or further injure her knee. "Ready when you are, Mom."

"I'm glad you're calling me Mom. I'm sorry if I'm crotchety."

Warmth flooded Cami's heart. Her mom had acknowledged

her feelings toward the more intimate name change? She apologized for her brisk mood? Delightful changes. "Mom—"

Her mother held up a hand. "I should have said this days ago, and I hope it's not too late. I'm glad you're helping me. You've been a tremendous support."

Cami blinked back happy tears. She couldn't recall the last time she'd heard approval and gratitude from her mom. "It's never too late to say kind words. I'm happy I can help."

"Though I'm glad I told your sisters to stay put, I'm thankful you're here for me."

"I am too." She helped her mom stand. "You okay?"

"I'll be fine, as long as I have you by my side."

Wow. Had this health scare awakened her mom that much that this whole new, tender side was now showing? Prayers answered?

"Mom, I'll always be here for you."

"Your father should be the one helping me."

"Don't worry. I'm attentive. Besides, Dad drove through the night from Cincinnati. He needed to sleep in this morning."

"He didn't have to do me any favors."

"Mom, Dad loves you. He is doing the best he can. And know what? I love you too." This expressing love was much easier than she had ever dreamed about.

"Oh, fine. I'm the one doped from medication and you're the one getting mushy."

Cami chuckled. "Come on, Mom. You know love doesn't hurt."

"Oh, Camille, love has hurt you. And I'm so sorry it has."

Todd.

She blinked away haunting images. "There were enough happy times together to hang my memories on. If given a choice, I'd marry Todd all over again, without a thought." That spoken confession made her whole being become the lightest and freest in years. "It's time to move on."

"I'm happy for you. Really, I am. I believe you're right about moving on in life, putting aside non-pleasant times." She pointed at the garage. "Whose car?"

Cami did a double take. She must have failed to notice the extra car when she'd pulled into the driveway. "It's Gavin's. He was with me when you were admitted to the hospital."

Her mom tightened her grip on Cami's elbow. "Of course. I remember. He's the one I ordered out of my hospital room. I can't believe he has the nerve to come to my house."

"Mom, seconds ago we were talking about displeasing events. You even said we must put those times aside in our minds. Can't you do that for Gavin and his family?"

"Yes. But we were talking about family, specifically your husband. Not this person."

"This family of ours got bent out of shape emotionally when we and the rest of the neighborhood badmouthed the Kinkaid family. We wanted to see them fall apart and disappear. Instead, we were the ones who fell apart and drifted away emotionally from each other. It's time to love and respect each other." Cami glanced at Gavin's car again then looked back at her mother. "He's quite concerned about you."

Amazement darted across her mom's eyes. "He is?"

"Theresa, dear," a shout came.

Cami glanced toward the house to see her dad standing at the front door. It never failed to amaze her how handsome Greg Hitchcock managed to look, even if rumpled from exhaustion. She signaled him over.

"Grandma," Danny shouted from the same spot where his grandfather stood seconds ago. He barreled toward them. "School's closed 'cause of a plumbing problem that made a big flood. Grandpa and I just finished breakfast."

"Easy, peanut butter cup." Cami put an arm around her son. "Let's get Grandma indoors, first."

Gavin stepped out from the house. Dressed in snug black

jeans and a thick white sweater pullover, he could make the biggest Hollywood star shudder.

"Oh, Mom," Cami said, pointing. "Look at the bouquet of flowers Gavin has for you."

"For me?"

"Well, this is your house. He's visiting you, not me. They must to be for you."

Her mother's lower lip twitched. "I'm not sure about this...this visit."

Cami couldn't resist the tease. "Are Gavin's hot looks overwhelming you?"

Her mom harrumphed and then slowly continued toward the house.

"Wait," Greg said. "You were just discharged. I'm helping you. No arguments." He flanked her left side. "Camille, you grab your mother's right arm." He looked tenderly at his wife and constant companion. "Together, we'll make sure you're just fine."

Inside, Gavin handed Theresa the flowers. "For you."

"Oh," she murmured. "Tulips. How lovely. Thank you."

Cami took the red and white flowers from her mom. "Where did you ever get these beauties this time of year? It's a touch of spring."

Gavin rubbed at the grin crinkling his mouth. "I have my sources."

She stood on her toes and kissed him on the cheek. He playfully rubbed at the spot, mouthing *wow*.

Danny bounced on his toes. "Mom kissed Gavin...Mom kissed Gavin."

Friendship or love? Cami wanted the real thing. But, she couldn't have it. She tightened her grip on the flowers, crackling the green cellophane wrap.

Greg eyed the stairwell in uncertainty. "Where to, Teri?"

Theresa's eyes widened. "You haven't called me Teri in years." She grimaced at the stairs. "I'll rest in the living room."

Cami sighed inwardly. The old gloom threatened to rush back and cloak her like the weight of a life-long sentence. Her thoughts drifted to yesterday's church service. Ah. She knew what God wanted her to do.

"Dad." She nudged her father in the side. "Go on."

His brows creased. "Pardon? I must have missed something."

"Tell Mom how happy you are to see her."

He rolled his bottom lip. "Well, I just rushed home from out of state. Just helped her indoors. Doesn't that say it all?"

She pressed a reassuring hand on her dad's arm. "Tell Mom how much you love her. And give her a hug."

"Love?"

Cami resisted rolling her eyes. "Yes, Dad. Love."

"You're right." With the fumbling movement of a nervous young man on his first date, her dad swung his arms around her mom's waist. "That's better." He kissed her on the lips. "I hurried home because I love you. Teri. I'm thankful you'll be healthy in no time. With that high blood pressure, thank God you didn't have a heart attack or stroke."

"Greg, is that really you or have you been replaced by an alien while in Cincinnati?"

"Grandma!" Danny said. "You're funny."

"Oh, dear. We sound like a big happy family. I need to sit down."

"Mom," Cami said in a trill. "We just may become a happy family."

"Let's make you comfortable." Her dad helped her mom to her favorite burgundy damask armchair.

"I better get a vase for these lovely tulips." Cami glanced at Gavin then winked at her mom. "The ones your tall and handsome admirer brought you."

❄

*A*lone in her mom's kitchen, tightness gnarled at Cami's heart. She found it difficult to believe Gavin had dropped by to visit with her folks only out of a token of friendship. Yet, they'd made an agreement the other day, a pact to appear often in public. A pledge to right the social wrongs of yesterday. And that's where the fisted feeling came from within; this constant longing for someone she knew who couldn't be hers wasn't easy to accept. One moment she was up, feeling high in hope, but the next second she turned droopy by the reminder that Gavin wasn't interested in exploring a relationship with her. Neighbors they were, and neighbors they'd be. If she put this foolish notion of a romance between them aside, considering the turbulent past they'd shared, she was lucky they even talked.

But, this ache? It burrowed its way through every cell in her body. She wanted something more with Gavin. Much more than mere friendship.

Get off of it. Move on. Why was she in the kitchen? Ah, yes. A vase. She fished out a dark blue one from the stash under the kitchen sink. The color would complement the lovely tulips and be sure to cheer her mom.

"Cami?"

She set the vase on the gray granite counter. Turning around she fluttered her lashes at Gavin who stood inches away. His mouth curled in a sweet and undeniably affectionate smile. A slight peppermint scent wafted up from those very lips she couldn't stop staring at.

He fanned his fingertips lightly across her cheek and then swept them to the nape of her neck. A delicious fire of excitement buzzed within her. Did he feel it too? She seized his fingers and pressed them back on her face. And dared not move.

"Cami, Cami," he said softly, his tone a gentle caress. "You've been away from us too long. Everything okay?"

Us. Not you've-been-away-from-me.

The kitchen door swung open. "Hey, Mom."

They faced Danny quickly as if they were two teenagers embarrassed to be caught together. Yet, they didn't sidestep away from each other. A nice thing. Did Gavin think that too?

"Grandma wants hot tea. Grandpa wants to know what's keeping you—he wants to talk with Gavin more about his watch collection before he leaves."

"Leaves?" Her one word came out heavy, like a dead weight pinning down her shoulders. She hadn't known Gavin would visit today, but now she didn't want him to go.

Gavin filled the vase with water from the tap. "Yes. I have to cram for a test."

"Did you goof off?" Danny asked.

Her son's playful but curious question shook Cami out of her daze. She tapped into the light mood. "Be careful with your answer, Gavin. My teacher-ears are listening."

"Well, chief, I've been awesomely busy with this cool dude and his mom the past few days. But I'll stay for a few minutes longer."

Danny pointed at his chest. "Me? Am I the cool dude?"

"You bet."

Danny whooped. "I'm gonna tell Grandma and Grandpa I'm a cool dude." He raced from the kitchen.

Cami and Gavin pivoted toward each other and erupted in chuckles.

She hugged her middle. "I love my boy."

"I do too."

Her heart fluttered. "You do?"

"Yes. Danny's a great kid. No surprise there with a great mom." He shook his head. "You know, the word *great* is an understatement when it comes to you."

She linked her fingers around the cross she'd started to wear again. "Your sweet words mean a lot to me."

He unwrapped the green plastic from the bouquet and

arranged the flowers in the vase. "I've been enjoying Friends with Danny and have put in extra hours this week. I'd like to share my thoughts with your family." His riveting gaze seized hers. The unspoken words were unmistakable. *You can trust me, Cami.*

She nodded; too dazzled by his voicing of his love for her son and thinking she was much more than great. She needed to hear this, needed to know. There she went again—hopeful and wishful for something that wouldn't happen. She sighed.

"Need help with anything?"

"No, thanks." She paused to drink in his handsome, oh so masculine face. "Go out with the rest. I'll make my mom tea and will be right out."

❄

*W*hen Cami joined the others a few minutes later with a tray of tea and ginger snap cookies she'd fished out from the pantry, she'd stepped into a twilight zone. Surely, she couldn't be seeing what played out before her eyes.

In the large, formal parlor with its elegant floor length curtains, bookcases stacked with both books and awards, and an antique rosewood grand piano, her dad and Gavin hovered over the corner table looking over Greg's pocket watch collection. They shared expressions of two men finding gems in a trinket shop. Anecdotes boomed from their rich voices. Seated at the settee, Danny nestled beside his grandmother, poring through a photo album on her lap. Danny turned the pages while asking questions Cami knew her son had longed to ask.

"How old was Grandpa when you first met him, Grandma?"

"We were both in our young twenties, Danny." She sighed dreamily. "It didn't take us a long time to fall in love."

The tray Cami held grew heavy. She set it down on the marble coffee table with a loud thud. "Refreshments anyone?"

"Goodness, Cami," Theresa clucked. "You rarely bring my

grandson over for a visit. Allow us to enjoy quality grandmother-grandchild time."

Cami smiled to herself. Yep, her mom's ever-ready rebuke reminded her that she was definitely in her parent's home, yet, with a delightful twist. Her mom wanted their company. For two people who were pros at secluding themselves from entertaining, both her parents were basking in this spontaneous get-together, appearing relaxed as if...

The five of them were a cohesive family.

"Gavin's staying for lunch," her mom stated, interrupting her musings.

Cami rubbed the back of her neck...the same spot where Gavin had touched her minutes ago back in the kitchen. This definitely wasn't like old times. Thank goodness.

"Camille, would you mind heating the casserole Gavin's mother prepared for us?" Theresa rubbed her belly. "My appetite is back full force and the promise of creamy chicken and biscuits is making my mouth water."

Cami peered at Gavin. "You're a man of gifts and surprises. Please give your mom a hug for me in appreciation." She nodded at the tray. "I guess we'll have the cookies I just brought out afterwards for dessert."

"Grandma," Danny said. "Did you know Gavin bakes awesome cookies?"

"Does he?" Theresa eyed Gavin. "From scratch?"

"That's the only way," Gavin answered. "I have a stash of old family recipes."

She smiled softly. "Then you must share them with me."

Cami turned to leave the room. Over her shoulder she took a peek at Gavin who had resumed chatting away with her dad. She smiled, praising God. How could she have ever doubted His presence in her life before?

14

*P*lanted at his desk with textbooks stacked in piles, the words disappeared, overtaken by images of Cami. Gavin pushed aside the current tome he was slogging through. Gorgeous, sunny, never-give-up Cami. Forget his cut and dry studies. She was the only thing he wanted to handle...wanted to wrap his arms around her and never let go. He longed to kiss her luscious lips, not surfacing until they knew intimately how to bring to each other the full joy that only two people in love knew from the inside out.

Cami.

In love?

What he always wished for, but knew he couldn't have?

Outside his window he caught sight of this woman preoccupying his thoughts as she pulled into her driveway. He glanced at the discarded textbooks, shrugged dismissively, and barreled downstairs. Happy, barking in pure puppy excitement, ran behind him to the door. "Sorry, pal. You stay here. A guy has to do what a guy does best."

He rushed across the road. "Hey, Cami."

"Hi, Gavin. You just can't get enough of us."

Although her tone was playful, he was dead serious. "Nope."

"This was some wonderful afternoon. You stayed with us longer than you'd planned."

"I had a great time."

She smiled wide. "Between me and Danny fussing over Mom, you talking watch-talk with Dad, and Danny boasting the truth about you two getting along at Friends and how we're good neighbors, the afternoon went splendidly. Although at first Mom tried to hold out on you, you obviously caused her to think twice."

He stepped closer. From the corner of his eye, he noticed a light flick on inside her house. Danny. He tamped down the desire to draw her into a hug.

"I hope your mom now sees me as less of a curse to society."

"Oh, that she does." Her smile faltered. "We did have a nice time together."

Her tone, noticeably strained, also troubled him. "I always have a nice time with you."

"You better go study, Gavin. Believe me, as a teacher and your neighbor, I'd hate to think I or my family was behind a failing grade on your exam tomorrow."

"And, as a friend?"

Her forehead knotted. "A friend?"

"Yes. A friend. A wonderful friend. What are you thinking, my friend?"

When she remained quiet, he cupped her face in the palm of his hands and did what his heart gave him no choice to do. He kissed her. Deeply and hungrily. The whole world could be watching for all he cared. He wanted her.

And she leaned into his kiss. Her desire matched his.

This was no little friendship between them.

He tasted lips sweet, warm, and accepting of his own. Sure, there was a sense of warmth, trust, and wholesomeness about her, but there was no mistaking he tasted a sampling of a pure pleasure awaiting them both...there for the taking, giving, and a forever sharing. If they wanted. And oh, he wanted.

He eased back, thinking about what he *wanted*, and how this wasn't the right time or place. Thinking he *wanted* to make the right time.

"I have to go."

"I understand." Her breath was choppy.

Yet, he lingered in hope she'd invite him into staying for a while. He could make this all G-rated and offer to cook her dinner...read a story with Danny...play with MJ the hamster. He'd do anything at this point to stay beside this woman he no longer wanted to be separated from. But—and wasn't there always an awful *but*—the logical half of his brain cautioned him to keep his distance. Less people to hurt. Less chances of getting hurt. Anguish had clobbered both of them over the head once too often.

He held his breath, waiting for her to continue. To say the words his heart desired to hear.

"Thanks for everything you've done, Gavin. You certainly helped to brighten Mom's day. Have a good night. Good luck with your studies."

Hitting the books? No way. Not with her on his mind.

"See you tomorrow," he stated more than he asked.

"Sorry. No can do. It's Open House at Little Bears and the day promises to be a long one. My folks are picking up Danny after school for a visit to their home. That's a first, and one I'm thrilled about."

"Well, okay then—until the next time. Good night."

She waved a goodbye and stepped indoors.

He breathed in deeply in an attempt to simmer his emotions. Not going to happen. Not as long as he saw her house, which of course couldn't be avoided. Not as long as he imagined the possibilities that life and love could encircle them both if they were part of each other's world.

But, evidently, some things were not meant to happen.

He hurried home, where he'd stick to his studies, after all. It was safer.

Once inside he jumped when three car doors slammed, rattling his front window.

He flung the door open. Three of his four sisters stood eye to eye with him.

"And the Wild West showdown begins," he said through gritted teeth.

15

"You bet it's a showdown, squirt," Denise said, her moon-gray eyes set hard on Gavin. "And we have you outnumbered. Don't even try coughing up an argument."

He leaned against the doorjamb. "I'd pray you came over for tea, but I'm thinking God's busy with a few other priorities."

His oldest sister, Diane, rolled her eyes. "Funny, not. Let's skip the God-talk. Move over, little brother. We're storming your house, like it or not." She took the lead. Denise and Donna followed, sticking to the pecking order by birth. Unfortunately, some family traditions never faded away.

Donna patted Gavin's left cheek. "You knew this was coming."

"Like a blizzard in February," he mumbled dryly under his breath. With little choice, he shut the door behind them and stepped into his living room. He deliberately flicked only one light on to illuminate his sisters. The shadowy atmosphere of the room didn't dim the thick tension between him and his uninvited guests, sisters or not.

Well, he knew what would crawl under their skin. He

wouldn't show an ounce of nervousness. Like a cat on the bottom of a scrap, he'd win this round.

He sat down on the recliner, leaned back, and folded his hands behind his head. He then plastered a grin on his lips. "This is my home. A home where God's invited to sit at the head of the table or beside me on the couch while I watch dumb sitcoms or whatever I choose. I won't hold back my love of God."

"You're a stinker," Diane said.

"Am I?"

Donna brushed the air with her hands as if separating two forces. "Enough sibling strife."

He must have gotten through to them if Donna, the family peacemaker, spoke up. Though she appeared lovelier than ever, rosy in both appearance and character with the expectancy of her first child's birth next month, she still chose to join the other two in ganging up on him. This was no intervention as if he needed to kick a substance abuse habit.

He summoned his manners. "Donna, have a seat. Don't tire yourself out on my account." He glanced at his other two sisters. "You too. We can discuss matters in a calm, mature fashion."

"I have my doubts," Denise muttered. She tended to be the most negative of the bunch.

"I'm surprised Deanna isn't with the three of you," he said, curious about their missing sister, and needing to deflect away from Denise's disposition.

"She would be but she's ill with the flu," Donna said.

He nodded appreciatively at the lack of bite in her words unlike Diane or Denise. "A shame. Hope it doesn't spread to her husband."

Denise smirked. "He's the one who got sick first and shared it. Listen, enough small talk. We have a major issue to talk about."

Gavin tucked the recliner back into its upright position. He flashed his best boyish grin. "What did I do now?"

Diane frowned. "Don't make this difficult. We have the family's best interest in mind."

He considered his studies, hating how their unplanned visit cramped his valuable time. "Narrow it down, please."

Denise, the only one who refused to sit began to pace. "This is about Pop." She pointed in the direction of Cami's house. "And her. Your neighbor."

He swallowed dryly. "She has a name. Cami Richardson. She's a fine neighbor."

"Cami, not Camille? A tad informal, are we? Or is the right word choice intimate? No matter. I know you remember well what she and those kids did to us years ago. And because of them, you couldn't possibly have forgotten our promise to Pop."

He willed any trace of frustration from his tone. "You did an awesome job refreshing my memory Saturday morning when you called." On his feet he shoved his hands into his jean pockets. "The operative word is *ago*. Years *ago* neighborhood kids picked on us, egged on by their parents because they didn't care for the way Mom and Pop chose to live. We know they had the means to fix and clean the place but chose not to. Instead, they put their time and energy into volunteer work, stuff folks outside the family never realized. And best of all, they fostered a good sense of family—we're a strong bunch." He cast each of his sisters with kindness. "Despite our differences, admit it, we love each other."

Diane nodded. "That's why we're here."

"But you're missing the essential point." He paused. "Mom and Pop chose to combat this problem by turning the other cheek —what God has taught us to do, although we as a family turned against our Heavenly Father." He crossed his arms. "Go figure, because I can't."

"But, the vow, Gavin. The vow," Denise pressed. "The elephant in the room that we can't ignore. Pop stopped turning the other cheek when he made each of us promise not to forgive the others. And that means Ms. Hitchcock."

"It's Richardson." He rubbed the back of his neck. "You want to know about a vow?" He paced beside Denise. "I made one—the only one that counts—to God."

Diane sighed. "It's back to that, huh?"

"It's always about God. I can't separate myself from Him," he said softly. "Listen, I can only pray one day you'll be able to respect me and my love for God. He loves each one of us. Including Cami and her son Danny." He turned to see his sister Donna hoisting herself from the soft-cushioned couch. She crossed the room toward him.

"We promised Pop to stay away from those kids, including Camille. It was a foolish and wrong pledge, but nevertheless we each swore to uphold this promise well into adulthood. Problems don't disappear unless they're resolved. The trouble is Pop doesn't see it like that. And, he's growing quite unhappy about the situation between you and your new neighbor or friend or whatever you prefer to call her."

"So, we need to do something to make Pop happy?"

All three sisters nodded.

He would have grinned if it weren't for the seriousness of the topic. "That *girl* has grown into a lovely married, now widowed, woman. I'm not just talking about looks, although she doesn't rate badly in that department either."

Denise groaned. "Ah. You do like her then? I've been worried about this."

Silence cloaked the room, pushing away attempts of dodging the one question that riddled his heart.

The word *like* no longer described his feelings for Cami. Not when he could still feel the indelible touch of her lips pressed against his, smell her heady scent that reminded him of a field of wildflowers, and see the beauty in her heart. Not when he couldn't stop thinking about her in his dreams or during each of his waking hours. Nor, did he want to. That passionate kiss he and Cami shared mere minutes before his Wild West gunslinging sisters showed up was still making his heart dance crazy.

No, he didn't simply like Cami. More like on the romantic, like she's-the-one level. He didn't think it was possible after Ariel.

He faced his sisters, unsure of where to begin his reply. He didn't need anyone's permission to fall for a specific woman.

Donna touched his arm. "Hey, squirt. We came to talk to you about Pop. He's pretty bummed. You know what it's like—if he's happy, we all are happy."

Gavin needed to take a stand against his family, for Cami. Later, he'd have to examine his heart and pray. God would guide him to the right woman if it were meant to be. He hoped he had His blessings on Cami.

Her voice replayed in his mind...she'd mentioned hosting an open house at Little Bears.

Diane pointed at Gavin. "You have this funny look in your eyes."

"I know that look," Donna said, her tone filled with tease. "Let's run for cover while we have a chance."

He held his hand up. "Hold it right there. Let's put you ladies to the test."

Denise winced. "Test? I've never been fond of that word."

"This one's easy. Just be yourselves."

"There's got to be a catch," Denise pressed.

He leveled his gaze at Denise then Diane. "You each have young children—and Donna has a baby on the way."

"Yeah?" Denise prompted. Nervousness twanged her tone.

"You love your children. You want the best for them. Correct?"

Both Diane and Denise nodded.

Donna rubbed her belly. "Definitely."

He smiled. Now he was getting somewhere. "Good. Then go meet Cami, the woman who she is today and not the kid from yesterday. Draw new conclusions and trash the old ones. Go see why she's an amiable, approachable person and why I think she's a fine woman."

Diane looked down her nose. "What are you suggesting?"

"Cami owns the preschool on North Boulevard, Little Bears. Tomorrow, she's hosting an open house for parents considering her childcare services. Meet the very changed Camille. See why I can't uphold our ridiculous vow to Pop and why he'll have to get over this." He uncrossed his arms. "We've all changed through the years. I believe it's safe to say that not one of us would like to be judged solely based upon what we did years ago."

Denise shuddered. "Pop doesn't get over things."

"With God's grace and our prayers he will move beyond this mess."

"God's grace..." Donna echoed.

Denise sighed loudly. "Donna, don't tell me you're thinking twice about God. If God existed, we wouldn't have been put into this mess."

Donna looked nervously at Gavin. He swung an arm around her while peering at his two other sisters.

"Let's be the one to forgive," he said. "It will start with us. We need to let the past stay in the past and live in the present."

Diane palmed the sides of her head. "Sounds too New Age for me."

He shook his head. "God wants us to enjoy life. He wants us to be kind and to love each other. We can't go wrong."

Donna squeezed him tighter to her. "You're going to be a great uncle."

Denise squirmed away and started for the door.

"Hey, sis," he called. "Do it for me."

Denise stopped short of the door but averted her eyes.

He tried again, searching for words his sister might relate to. "Cami is a wonderful, strong woman, overcoming her own set of childhood hurdles." He aimed for his sister's heart. "And like you, she's also a single mom, works hard and loves her child fiercely."

Denise curled a strand of hair around a finger. "Does she want a reward?"

"No," he said with a level voice, refusing to get ruffled by is sister's sarcasm. "Have compassion, sis. Cami is kept hostage by tons of guilt over those childhood antics. She's walked around for years with that guilt wearing her down because she knows she shouldn't have banded with the others against us. She's totally different than the girl you once knew. We need to forgive her. Go visit tomorrow. See for yourselves."

Denise blinked twice. "Fine. For you, I'll go."

He released a pent-up breath.

"I don't know what to do about Pop," Denise added.

"God will handle Jake Kinkaid. I'm putting my trust in Him. How about you?"

"I will," Donna said.

"Faith in God sounds like the only option," Diane said. "With God working to remove the grizzly out of Pop then there's more of a reason for us to try."

They shared smiles. His sisters left after a round of kisses and hugs.

Upstairs awaited a pile of books and notes for a heavy-duty cramming session, though he doubted his concentration abilities. Cami. Was she smiling? Keeping warm in this cold temperature? Unexpected warmth chased the last of the chill from his veins as he wondered if she was lonely for his company.

"*Y*ou did what?" Cami placed the last tray of homemade baked treats for her open house carefully into her car trunk and faced Gavin. "Please tell me I misheard."

"After we parted yesterday, my sisters paid a visit."

Despite the single-digit December temperature, sweat trickled down her back. The pressure to arrive at work early to prepare for the long day she faced intensified upon hearing this news. She'd be lucky if she could muster half a smile for the parents visiting today while trying to quash the butterflies already fluttering in her belly over meeting Gavin's sisters.

She unfastened the top button of her coat. "I don't understand. Your family despises me. In their eyes I'm the nasty Hitchcock girl who bullied you guys and am forever doomed."

"They each have preschoolers except for Donna, who has a baby on the way. They've been looking for a good day-care center and I thought—"

"That they should check me and Little Bears out?"

He gently stroked her left cheek, running his fingertips in a cascade toward her chin. Flashes of yesterday floated before her. His kiss. His sweet mouth firmly pressing upon hers, absorbing her into him, making them become one. She didn't pull away. Didn't want to. Instantly, her cares and worries vanished. He'd reassured her everything would be good, and she had believed him. She didn't want that kiss to ever end, wanted to always be in his arms. She had trusted him then. She needed to trust him now.

He inched closer, sealing off the cold wind between them, and bringing her back to the present. "That's exactly my idea," he murmured into her ear. "I told them how wonderful you are." He enveloped his warm hands around her cold fingers. "I told my sisters it's time they forgave you by putting those troubling times behind us and moving on with our lives."

She peered into his gentle eyes. Already weary of showing others that their friendship wasn't about to cause havoc in the community, her pulse quickened. She wanted a real relationship with him. They were either falling in love with each other or not. But if she pressed Gavin like she'd pushed Todd, she chanced sending him bolting to a place of no return.

She shuddered. "Your sisters will grind me to a pulp and spit me out like a sour taste."

His eyes smiled in that twinkly way of his when determination marched as his partner. "No they won't."

"How do you know?"

"I know my sisters. And I know you. They'll see you as sincere, loving, giving, and most trustworthy. You're everything good."

A chill poked her spine. Those weren't exactly romantic words. Nice words, sure, but they described a good person. And she wanted him to think of her as more than simply nice, more than the girl next door. Her heart drooped; she slumped forward. He saw her no differently than other good people. This wasn't exactly what she'd been dreaming of tucked in bed last night. Apparently, it circled back to showing their families and the community nothing bad would happen because they chose to be friends. Friends. Nothing more.

But, then there were his touches. His kiss.

Her wanting more. Much more.

He wouldn't go around kissing her like he had if he didn't feel something more powerful. The dates she'd had before meeting and marrying Todd had taught her this lesson the hard, hurtful way. There was definitely a difference between passionate love and passionate lust.

On the other had, one thing stood out clearly. He wasn't coming right out and talking about taking their *friendship* into the next level. An intimate relationship didn't exist, presently and most likely, never would. It was what it was. All things considering, she should be grateful to have this peace between them.

She patted her coat pocket for her keys. "Well, looks like I have everything. I'll be late if I don't get on my way."

"So, you're good with my sisters?"

"You're right. There's nothing I need to be ashamed of. Besides, I have a business to run, a service to offer." She smiled. "And a good one."

His brow furrowed. What reply had he expected?

She took a step to the driver's side.

"I'll call you tonight to see how things went."

"No problem."

But, she had a problem. She'd liked Gavin in a way far more than he cared for her. She'd have to steel herself toward him. One shattered heart in a lifetime had been more than enough for her. Not again.

She'd have to face the Kinkaid sisters, stand tall in confidence, not disgrace. Somehow.

With God. That was how. Yet, she was trembling.

16

*C*ami glanced at the clock on her office wall and jabbed at the knot between her eyes. Ten o'clock. Not one Kinkaid sister had walked through Little Bears' door. Could she dare believe she might be off the hook and relax? A knock at the door, making her jump, nixed that foolish notion. "Yes?"

Colleen, one of her teachers and dear friends, poked her head into the room. "Is something wrong?"

"Everything's fine."

"Right. As fine as a child-meltdown during naptime." Colleen came forward. "Come on, spill it."

Cami shuffled a stack of papers. "I'm just looking for a consent form."

Her friend placed a caring hand on her shoulder. "You've been a bundle of nerves this morning. Your smiles can't hide the truth from me."

Cami unburied the forms on her desk. When she reached for it, she snared the paper clip binding the pile with other papers. The stack flew to the floor.

"Figures."

"Hey gal, forget the papers. Let's talk."

"Not with the place packed with parents and their excited children."

"You've faced plenty of Little Bear visitation days so I know that's not the number one thing upsetting you. Everything's under control and you know it. You wouldn't have ducked out to your office, otherwise. Monica and Tina have their kids painting. Annie and Kathy are storytelling. Luck's on our side today—our two mom-volunteers are recovered from the flu and helping out with sleeves rolled high. But, you aren't yourself, and I want to know why."

Cami ran a fingertip along the silver chain of her cross to remind her whom she could always lean on. "You're right. There's a chance for some guests stopping by this morning to observe the center."

Her friend made a funny, sweet face. "That's what an open house is about, honey—inviting others to observe us at work. You've never been out of sorts during one of these before. Now, if it were bankers about to foreclose—"

"No need to worry. We're in fine financial shape. It's just these three sisters who might pay a visit today, well, it's as if they're stepping right out of my past."

"A past you don't want to revisit?"

She nodded, relieved Colleen knew her well enough not to press for every detail, especially with an uncomfortable subject.

"You're a good woman. Remember, each one of us has something we're troubled by." Colleen pointed to herself. "I definitely do. Look below the surface veneer most people use as a shield and you'll see flaws or bad times or both. None of us are innocent or are lucky enough to escape rough times."

Colleen was right. Cami knew she didn't inhabit a perfect world. Again, she reached for her cross, this time cradling the silver pendant in her palm.

"I have to get out to the children, but wanted to check on you." Colleen paused at the door. "You'll be fine. I know you will."

"Thanks. You're a true kindred spirit."

"Come along, sweets. You're the star of this place."

"You're kind, but at Little Bears we're each a star." Cami stood tall, straightening her brown corduroy skirt and her while pullover sweater. "With God's love all is possible, including harmony among enemies." She smiled, surer in her heart. "Let's go. You're right—everything will be fine."

"Said like the true trooper you are."

Cami past the other two offices, the kitchen, lunchroom, and restrooms then entered the main room. Upon seeing the children happy and energetic, she released her first relaxed breath of the day. Plus, smiling parents filled the place. New prospective clients snacked on the refreshments and coffee. The staff appeared calm. She couldn't ask for a thing more.

From the corner of her eye, she caught a glint reflecting through the large window facing the road. A car pulled into the parking lot. Three women quickly got out of the car, one whose unbuttoned navy blue coat revealed an expectant mom-to-be belly.

Her breath snagged between her lungs and throat. The sisters had arrived.

I have it under control. I'm a decent person. God is on my side.

I can do this.

"Mrs. Richardson," a child said, yanking on her skirt.

"Yes, Brandon?"

"Mommy wants to see my fire truck picture."

She smiled. "That's a great painting. Your mommy will like it a lot. Let's find it."

The rosy-cheeked boy grasped her hand. She had a school to oversee. She didn't have time to fret over potential clientele, Gavin's sisters or anyone else. These women were not a firing squad that she was destined to stand before. As long as she continued to give her best to her pupils and staff she'd be fine.

Ten-thirty. It was time for a round-circle activity. Cami helped her staff assemble the *cubs* into a large circle for one of their favorite games. Fifteen minutes later, before small attention spans broke, the large circle broke into five smaller ones for more group activities. At eleven-thirty, she glanced at the ever-changing mixture of adult observers.

There was no mistaking the three Kinkaid sisters. They and their brother shared distinct Kinkaid features, from their beautiful sparkling gray-blue eyes to wide, brilliant smiles.

Smiles?

She glanced again. They were hovering over the refreshment table, smiling and conversing with the other parents. Not one of them appeared ready to cast daggers her way. A sigh of relief escaped from her lips. Hope. How nice that felt.

Lunchtime arrived just in time before any child became irritable. Cami helped wash the kids' hands and seat them at their children-sized lunch tables. She answered a question from one of the moms about the meals. Colleen and Tina distributed grilled cheese sandwiches, carrot sticks, and apple juice. When she glanced away for a moment, she saw the Kinkaid sisters leave with Brandon's parents. She had a hunch they were leaving for lunch and detailed conversation and would return afterwards.

One o'clock rolled along and brought music time. The teachers corralled the cubs around Annie to sing along as she played her guitar. That's when the Kinkaid sisters returned.

"Mrs. Richardson, Shanna took my doll."

Cami hunkered down to be at the girl's eye-level. "Let's see what we can work out with Shanna. We share our toys, sweetie."

The girl nodded and they walked over to Shanna, the notorious doll-thief of the group. Another crisis thwarted.

Half past one o'clock spelled naptime. The staff unrolled the children's blankets and floor mats and settled them down for their afternoon sleepy-time naps. Cami started to circulate among the parents, thanking them for attending the open house.

"I'll be happy to answer anyone's questions," she said to the remaining parents. "Let's step nearer my office so we don't disturb the little ones."

Brandon's mother approached. "We have to meet someone at the shop before we pick up our little boy. Thanks for another impressive day. You run a delightful place."

Cami thanked the mother who was on a first-name basis with her. In addition to Brandon, her three other children had been enrolled in Little Bears through the years.

Brandon's father shook her hand. "Thanks for hosting an open house today. It's good to know my son's in good, capable hands."

"My goodness, how nice of you to say. Thank you."

She spent the next few minutes answering questions, thanked departing guests, and invited the others to enjoy a freshly brewed pot of coffee.

Now or never. Cami turned to face the sisters. "Welcome. I saw you earlier, but haven't had a chance to say a personal hello." She shook each of their hands. "I'm Cami Richardson and I'm glad you're here. We certainly had a big crowd today."

The oldest-looking of the three nodded, but remained silent. Cami wiped her sweaty hands on her sides.

The pregnant one, whose facial features were a near perfect match to Gavin, approached. "Hello, Cami. I'm Donna Pedrowski. These are my sisters Diane Carter and Denise Finney. I don't know whether you remember us from school since we were a few years ahead of you, but you were in the same class as our brother, Gavin. Gavin Kinkaid."

"Honestly," Cami said as she looked at each sister, "I don't recall the three of you individually, but definitely know of your family as a whole. I do see a distinct Kinkaid resemblance." She easily pushed out the other words itching to make a leap. "Gavin's my next door neighbor, though you must be aware of that." The mere mention of Gavin's name comforted her like a double rainbow after a thunderstorm.

Diane and Denise paled. Donna shifted her hands from on top of her belly to under then back above. Cami knew of only one thing to do to quell their nervousness. She'd treat these women like other potential clientele, with cordiality.

She smiled, aiming to place a hum in her tone. "Tell me, ladies, do you have children you're considering enrolling in Little Bears?"

Diane spoke fondly of her twin daughters who recently turned four. With each description of the girls, her rigid posture relaxed and her facial features brightened. Denise then shared several funny anecdotes about her three-and-a-half-year and two-year-old boys. "I know for a fact that my sons' single goal is to never sleep, or let me enjoy rest."

They all chuckled before she turned serious.

"As a single mom I'm drained from full-time work and parenting. A little relief in the form of a place where I can trust my sons will be taken care of sounds like paradise."

"Oh, I understand where you're coming from," Cami said softly. "The mission statement of Little Bears is to provide comfort to both child and parent."

Denise smiled. "Good to know."

Cami faced the youngest of the sisters. "And you, Donna? Do have other children or will this be your first?"

Donna gently patted her belly. "My first. And, if little David Jr. doesn't stop jabbing my ribs, he may be my only."

Cami put her arms around Donna, trying to ignore Diane and Denise's lifted brows and scrunched foreheads. "I hate to tell you how often I've heard this, sweetie. Good thing we forget as soon as we set our eyes on our precious babes."

Donna gave her sisters a sideways glance then faced Cami. "You sound just like my sisters and mom. I'd love to stay home until the baby's old enough for kindergarten, but I need to help my husband financially."

"It's not easy these days."

All three sisters bobbed their heads.

"We're quite impressed with the place," Donna said. "At lunch we agreed you put your heart into caring for these kids like they were your own."

"Aw, thank you. That's nice to hear." They talked more. Cami easily answered their questions and dealt with concerns.

"At Little Bears your children are in excellent hands. My teachers are certified and believe me, before they start I know then inside and out."

"You and your staff present yourselves as friends and professionals," Denise said. "To tell you the truth, I've never encountered this quality combination in the day-care centers I've visited. I like the stress-free environment it fosters."

"It must be a plus for the children," Diane said. "I've seen enough and have plenty to think about. Let's go Denise and Donna."

"You two go out to the car. I'll meet you in a minute or two," Donna said.

Denise eyed Donna suspiciously then nodded, and exited the building with Diane.

"How can I help you?" Cami asked.

Donna fiddled with her blouse collar. "I'd like to speak with you about my brother."

Cami summoned calm with a deep breath. "Let's step into my office. While the kids are napping, I have a few minutes to spare."

"That would be wonderful. Thank you."

They moved into Cami's office. She motioned for Donna to have a seat.

"Thanks. This baby is already tiring me out."

Cami sat at her desk chair opposite of Donna. "Mrs. Pedrowski, you mentioned a desire to talk about Gavin?"

"Please, call me Donna."

"And again, please call me Cami."

"I guess I should get right to the point," Donna said, but didn't say a word more.

Cami nodded in encouragement.

Donna leaned back. "There's not much to dislike about you."

"And that's a disappointment?"

A little grin spread across Donna's lips. "I like you, Cami. And, to be more candid, you aren't the person I expected."

"Do you mean like the girl I used to be?"

Donna lowered her lashes. "Yes."

"Most of us change from childhood, learning from our mistakes. I pity those who don't."

"You're right. Listen—to get to my point and not keep you longer—Gavin has already told us you're sorry you went along with the other neighborhood kids. When you think about it, we were all to blame."

"I'm not following."

"We surely didn't stick up for ourselves, nor did we go out of our way to try to make friends with you guys. You picked on us and we reacted by staying away, probably encouraging more bullying. It was a vicious cycle, both sides feeding off each other."

Cami folded her hands. "I believe that says it well. It takes two to fight."

"My sisters and I have another motivating factor for coming here in addition to our children needing quality care and that's because we love our brother dearly."

Cami waited quietly.

"We promised our father back when this transpired to keep away from you and the others. Forever. Now Pop's getting red under the collar that you and Gavin are...are..." Donna began to fan her face with her hand.

"Friends and neighbors."

"Honestly, your relationship shouldn't matter to us as long as you're kind to each other. You're adults. What happened back then got out of control, on both sides. It should be forgotten about, or at least, put aside. We need to move forward."

"I agree, Donna. In the name of love, it's time to forgive each other. I don't know how to remedy the wrong I've done to your family. I'm trying my best to run a decent business, to raise my own son in a way that he'll be respectful to others, to..."

Donna held up a hand. "There's no need to justify your actions. My pop's the one carrying on a grudge. Honestly, my sisters and I too, right up to today. I believe our hearts and attitudes are softened for the best. Certainly two wrongs don't make a right. Pop needs to forgive others as well as himself. He's a great dad, but sometimes he can be a little hardheaded."

"How does Gavin stand about this promise to your father?"

"He thinks we should trust God and let Him see to Pop."

"Donna, do you believe in God and that He can take care of this mess?"

"Truthfully, my relationship with God is like a diet. A lot of yo-yoing on and off."

Cami softly smiled. "I know where you're coming from. Funny, how we easily find solace in God when things go right, but not when life tilts in the wrong direction."

"That is the sad truth, for sure."

"Your brother has been a fine neighbor. He's brought me back to church, helping me to end my oscillating faith, which I'm grateful for. He's been a terrific buddy for my son at the Friends program. But, that's about it between us."

Donna shook her head.

Little pinpricks tickled Cami's arms. Hope and excitement?

"I know my brother. I know when he's falling in love with someone."

A flush heated Cami's face. "Love? Between Gavin and I?"

Donna smiled. "I like you, Cami. I think in time my whole family will get to know you and will like you as if you've been a family member from the get-go. I wonder how we can hasten this slowpoke rate."

"I like you too, Donna. But, I think you're mistaken about me and Gavin."

Donna shifted in her seat. "I don't know about that. The Kinkaid men love fast and hard, with their all."

"Fast and hard," Cami echoed.

"Yes, both Pop and Gavin"—Donna thumped her chest—"absorb life right through their hearts. When it comes to love, watch out. They don't bend easy."

"Love, huh?" Cami rubbed at a smile. "I just thought of something."

"Yes?"

"Let's unite our families at church for the Christmas Eve service next week. Instead of worrying, let's put our confidence in God and see what His capable hands will do. He knows our hearts' desires."

"Sounds like a fine plan. I'll manage one way or another to get my whole family there. God will help." Donna struggled to raise herself and stopped when Cami walked around from the desk and offered a helping hand.

The two women stared at each other then pulled the other into an embrace.

"This has been a fine starting point," Cami said. They arranged for the time to meet for the church service and Cami walked Donna out to the main entrance of the building.

Afterwards, she returned to the main room to find her sleepy-head cubs stretching and yawning and asking for a snack. Soon, they'd be hopping with a frenzy of energy.

Wait until she arrived home from work later on to tell Gavin what happened. He'd be happy, especially about bringing their families together at church.

About to join the others, she stopped short. Could Donna be right about Gavin falling in love with her? Did she love him? Had she loved him all these years? Could she trust another man with her heart after losing her husband? She rubbed between her eyes. What difference did any of these answers make? He only wanted to be friendly neighbors. Looks like she'd never know when it comes to trusting him about this thing called love.

inally home from work, Cami slid out from her car. The long day had more ups than downs, more laughs than stresses. Not bad at all. Although wiped out energy wise, gratitude and a sense of serenity lightened her footsteps.

With Danny visiting with his grandparents, she wondered if Gavin would be receptive to coming over for a visit. She wanted to share the good news about what she and Donna planned. Afterwards, when Gavin returned home and Danny came back, she'd fix a lazy meal of burgers and fries followed by lots of cuddling with her son over a treat of a DVD and popcorn then an early bedtime for both of them. That was everything perfect.

The distinct sound of snow crunched by heavy boots came from behind. She turned around and smiled. "I was just thinking about you."

"And I was thinking about you." He wore a new jacket, a blue ski-style one that suited his dark hair and handsome features. Happy, the adorable pup, wiggled in his arms.

Unable to resist, she reached out and scratched between his ears. She was rewarded by an exuberant bark and lots of tail wagging. "Hey there, you look as if you could tackle any snow-covered mountain."

Happy mouthed Gavin's hand. "You little sneak." He playfully roughed the puppy up and glanced warmly at Cami. "Did you mean me or Happy conquering that mountain?"

She laughed. "Both."

"When I saw you pull up, I decided to walk over instead of phone. How did it go today?"

"Fine. Come in for a hot drink and I'll tell you about it. Happy is welcomed too."

His eyes widened. "Yes. We'd like that."

While Cami put water up to boil for their chocolate-raspberry cocoa and dug out an old toy of Danny's to gift Happy, she pondered whether she should mention Donna's admission of the pledge Gavin and his sisters made to their father all those years ago. When he began to whistle a favorite show tune of hers, she decided not to ruin a light mood. Besides, it wasn't her place to bring it up.

His whistle ceased. She glanced under the kitchen table where Happy lay contently on the red and brown braided rug with his new chew toy between his paws. Her gaze returned quickly to Gavin who sat straight with relaxed shoulders. A charming grin tugged at his lips.

"What are you thinking, Gavin?"

"Happy looks like he belongs here, huh?"

That puppy wasn't the only one who appeared as if he belonged in the same house as her. Despite her agreement to keep the status qou between them on the friendship level, it was impossible to deny how the sight of him stirred her. "Oh, yeah," she murmured.

His sister's words wagged before her. *I know my brother...I know when he's falling in love with someone.*

Cami's heart pounded. Yes, she admitted to herself, unable to deny, disguise, or brush aside the truth a second longer. She'd fallen in love with Gavin. And that was the awful problem since he wasn't offering anything more than neighborly love.

The kettle hissed. She stood and turned off the rattling pot of water.

"Cami," he murmured from beside her. She hadn't been aware of when he'd stood or stepped beside her. He covered her fingers draped over the kettle handle. Close enough that she could turn and snuggle into his arms and soak up his warmth, his strength, and his protectiveness, as if they were one. Close enough to share kisses, making each new one more special than the previous one.

If he wanted to.

She wanted to.

"I'm concerned about you," he said, his voice a tender balm to her kaleidoscope feelings. "You've been standing with the kettle turned off for a minute or two, staring off into space. What's on your mind?"

You.

Us. If there is such a thing.

She shook her head, trying to clear her thoughts, but knew she couldn't. Not with him a whisper away.

"Sorry. How rude of me." She looked at his hand holding hers. She really had to end the guessing games between them. "I...uh—"

"Go sit," he said. "You're tired from a long day at work. I'll mix the cocoa. You rest."

She didn't want to step away from him. She didn't want to talk about her day. At that given moment, the only thing she wanted was the one thing she couldn't have...to be with him, forever.

"You're silly," he said affectionately. He placed his hands on her shoulders and gently guided her toward a kitchen chair. "I hope my sisters didn't upset you."

"Oh, no, not at all. The two older ones were pleasant, although reserved. Then Donna and I chatted in my office."

"On a one-on-one?" he said, sounding impressed. "I can't imagine Donna saying anything troubling."

"I believe we hit it off well. Actually, we have a"—she made air quotes—"scheme going between us."

He brought the steaming mugs over to the table and sat down beside her. Again, only a mere space between them existed. She wished for zero distance separating them.

"I'm listening."

"To unite our families under one church roof Christmas Eve."

"And to show my family you and Danny aren't horrible people, and likewise, your family would have a chance to get to know my family more?"

She nodded, sheepishness making her drop her gaze downward.

He reached out and tucked her cold hands into his warm ones. "You're a beautiful, beautiful woman, Cami. That's really not a scheme. Just a great plan."

She shook her head.

He lifted her chin for their gazes to connect. "Look at me, honey. I wouldn't ever tell you something that isn't true."

She batted her eyes. One thing she did know about Gavin and admired was that he wouldn't lie to her.

"I'm going to level with you. This entire friendship-only idea of ours is wrong. I'm sorry I ever suggested this line of action. We're two mature adults who no longer have to be ashamed of our actions. What we should have done upfront is to plainly unite our families. It's brilliant you and Donna thought of this. And the plan to bring them together in church, worshipping God on Christmas Eve, is excellent. There's something more, though."

"Yes?"

The back kitchen door banged open. They both jumped.

Danny pushed shut the door behind him. He stared at Gavin. "What are you doing here?"

Cami sprang from her seat. "Danny, what's wrong?"

Danny didn't look away from Gavin. "Nothing's wrong with me. It's him."

She frowned. This couldn't be her loving, cute, little boy behaving antagonistically. She glanced at Gavin. A look of bewilderment furrowed his brows.

She stepped toward Danny, reaching out to him.

"No," he cried out. "I don't like Gavin anymore."

"Danny, please tell me what—"

"I'm out of here," Danny muttered and ran past her. His stomping on the stairs echoed seconds later through the otherwise still house.

She crossed her arms, hugging them tight around her middle. "I don't understand."

Gavin tucked her into his embrace. "Me either. I thought everything went smoothly yesterday at your folks' house."

"It's been good at Friends?"

"Absolutely," he said, backing his affirmation with a nod.

"That's not like Danny."

"Maybe it's a kid-thing. They go through quite a few phases, not that I need to tell you."

Unable to remain in his arms with an angry child upstairs, she stepped back. She needed to get to the bottom of this, and fast. "There's no excusing Danny's rudeness and I apologize. I've raised my son to know that in this household when he's troubled we talk out our problems in a calm and respectful way."

He stepped back, his hands falling to his sides. "I should go."

She wished he could stay, wished they both could erase the last few minutes from history. He had called her honey only seconds before Danny's peculiar arrival home. He'd made her feel accepted, treasured, and dare she believe, loved.

"It's probably for the best. I'll call you."

He reached out to her then halted. He hoisted Happy into his arms then turned toward the door. Again, he paused. Slowly, he turned to face her.

"If it brings you comfort to know, I'll be praying for the two of you."

His words reminded her of the first time he spoke those words. Then, she'd been amazed he wanted to pray for her after years of trouble between them. Now, his prayer comforted her, bringing a gentle reminder that God would watch over them. One way or another, everything would be fine.

"Thanks, Gavin. Yes, knowing you'll be praying for us does bring great comfort."

"Call me."

"Definitely," she said, and watched him leave.

She bowed her head. "Father, I know you're in the driver's seat and I'm thankful. Where to from here?" Without a second more delay, she approached the stairs. Though God would oversee to her needs, the stairwell leading toward Danny's bedroom looked long and rickety.

*G*avin wished Cami a good night and disconnected the phone. Six-thirty and she still didn't have a clue to why Danny had spewed the sudden beef with him and then slipped into an unnatural sullen state. The boy's unexpected behavior stung. Maybe he was overreacting, but he'd felt as if he'd received a one-way ticket to anywhere but next door to Cami and her son.

He groaned.

Yep. That was how much he cared for those two.

Scratch that. He *loved* them.

His gaze roamed to the kitchen table where he'd left the unopened UPS delivery box. Inside awaited the parts he'd ordered for his joint holiday project with Danny. Serious doubts jabbed his mind that this task would get accomplished. Well, it was time for a change and he would make it happen. Fast. If it meant taking a chance on a kid with a grudge, and confronting his own stubborn father, then no one was going to get in his way.

Twenty minutes later he pulled into his folks' driveway and greeted his mom as he entered the kitchen door.

"Hello, son." She gave him a big hug. "This is an unexpected but wonderful visit."

Gavin inhaled deeply. His mom's stew. His mouth watered and he swallowed hard. Pushing past his anguish, he forced a wide smile though it contrasted his mood. "Mmm. Where's the nearest fork?"

"As if you didn't know." His mom tapped the wooden spoon on the pot's rim then set it on a spoon rest. "You're welcome to have dinner with us, but one look at you says loud and clear you have other matters on your mind."

He restrained a sigh. "Ah, Mom, I could never keep things from you."

"Come sit. Tell me about what's troubling you." She gestured toward the kitchen table and chairs, where they'd sat plenty of times and talked about life's mysteries and confusion.

He stayed put and fished out the small kit from his coat pocket and laid it out flat on his palm. "I can't chat a second longer. I need to use Pop's shop before he…"

"Before your father arrives home from work?"

There was no sense in holding back from his mom. "Yes and no. To tell you the truth, I'd hoped to avoid Pop. Right up to seconds ago, I was still banking on missing him. But, now? If this confrontation is meant to be, then let it happen."

She wiped her hands on a nearby towel and squinted at his hands. "What's this mechanical-looking apparatus?"

His mom's off-topic question didn't escape his attention. She always knew what she was doing. He shoved the brass and steel mechanism back into his pocket. "The workings for a music box. It's a project I'm sort of involved in."

"Sort of?"

He rubbed the back of his neck.

"Would you like to sit a short spell and tell me about it?"

"Okay, but only for a minute. I'll like to cut the wooden box in Pop's shop and get back home. It's getting late."

She sat and motioned for him to sit beside her. "Pop's been working overtime this week. Today's no different."

His gut tightened. Nonsense. What had he just uttered to his mom? No way would he allow Jake Kinkaid to intimidate him.

He sat and his mom grasped his hands.

"Pop loves you, son. He's not a big bad wolf. He might growl every now and then, but he won't bite. Tell me about this music box. I'd think it's probably a good starting point."

He nodded. "It's actually part of the problem. Danny was excited about making a music box for his mom to replace the one she'd broken. He planned on it being his Christmas present for her. It's also part of Danny's Friends project."

"How thoughtful."

"Together, we pored over catalogs to select the right tune and find the drum and cone devices to produce the desired sound."

"Sounds perfect and meaningful. Cami will love it."

He reached for an apple from a bowl in the center of the table and polished it on his shirt. After a couple mouthfuls of the sweet fruit, he said, "Would have been fine, but for some unknown reason, Danny came home from school this afternoon on the war-path with me."

"Danny wouldn't reveal anything to his mom?"

He shook his head. "How's he been in school?" He bit into another section of apple.

"On the quiet side, unusual for him. I've been watching him carefully."

He pitched the apple core into the waste pail beside the sink and grabbed a napkin from the country-style basket. "Danny's told Cami he wants to disassociate from me. We don't get it. I haven't said a peep to hurt the boy. She's giving him lots of breathing space, in hope of getting to the bottom of this."

His mom squeezed his hand. "Mothers have a special knack for getting out the truth."

He grinned. "Like now."

"Because I love you, son." She leaned closer. "Do you think Danny's behavior is connected to Pop? Is Danny's action stoking your reluctance to see your father?"

"Million-dollar questions. But, I do know—from the sister brigade—Pop's exact views about my association with Cami. Not good."

"Ah, your sisters visited."

"They sure did. I invited them to attend Cami's open house at Little Bears and to see for themselves how wonderful of a person she now is."

"You're a smart one." She rubbed her hands. "Tell me what's up between you and Cami. I won't be fooled with you saying you're just good neighbors. There's something more."

He leaned back and stared.

"Don't look amazed. I know my children."

"Yeah, there is something developing between Cami and me."

His mom waited.

He sighed. He hated gaps in conversation. "I like Cami."

"Like?"

"Okay. You got me." He paused to lasso in his swirly emotions. Cami was doing one huge number on him...on his mind...on his heart. "Much more than like. But, this whole past-history between us, Danny's odd behavior, and Pop's attitude is spinning my head like crazy."

"Your broken engagement with Ariel must be a damper on things too."

Unable to speak, he nodded.

"Love is powerful stuff, son. It controls us 24/7 and we're at its mercy."

His mouth dropped. "Love? I didn't say—"

She interrupted him with a shake of her head. "You have to follow your heart."

It was back to the heart thing.

He glanced at his watch. Eventually Pop would arrive home tired, hungry, and wanting to get away from the world and its demands before he sat down for his evening meal. Often, that meant unwinding in this beloved wood shop and puttering a bit. Tonight, he sure wasn't in the mood for a Pop encounter.

He stood and kissed his mom.

She touched her cheek and smiled. "What's that for?"

"For being who and what you are—awesome. But what will truly help right now is going out to the shop and making this case."

"For Danny? A boy who doesn't want..." She fluttered her fingers across her mouth.

"Want anything to do with me? Yep. However, I have the parts and they won't do any good collecting dust."

After a hug, Gavin stopped at his car to retrieve the crate containing the special wood he'd also ordered for the music box then hurried to the shop.

A former old summer-kitchen, Pop had converted it to a shop for tinkering back when Gavin was ten and had expressed an interest in woodworking. Those were the days. He and his pop were inseparable. Time had a funny way of changing things.

He headed first to the wood stove that his mom had lit when she arrived home from work, a daily routine of hers during the workweek. He held out his hands to warm from the cold day before gathering scrap wood to beef up the low burning fire.

Plenty had changed since the time when he helped his father plan and build this shop. Life really began to spiral downhill when the neighborhood kids trashed the family, as if they belonged in the dark shadows of life and not deserving like others. Of course, now an adult, he saw through this nonsense, but it wasn't a surprise that he and his sisters had followed Pop's lead in turning away from God. No wonder forgiveness and moving forward in life had taken a setback. It wasn't until he'd joined the Air Force and then afterwards volunteered with Big Brothers Big Sisters in New York did he invite God back into his life.

And, his Heavenly Father opened His arms wide for him.

At the bandsaw he withdrew from the wood crate the pieces of walnut for the case and the spruce for the soundboard. Next, he pulled out from his shirt pocket the plans he and Danny had drawn together. But, slipping out with the paper came the memories from just last week with Danny at Friends...

"Gavin, will we get the wood in time?"

"Absolutely, chief. When I phoned in the order, the service representative assured me he'd express the order right away, despite the holiday season."

"Cool." Danny frowned. "But, that means we'll have to hurry. Mom might think that this is nothing special."

He patted the boy's shoulder. "When your mom sees this present of yours, she won't think about those kinds of particulars. Trust me on this one. She'll love this gift."

"I do trust you. You're the best. And, you're right. Mom will love the music box."

"I'm glad. I trust you as well."

"Wow." Danny smiled from ear to ear. "I'm just a kid, though."

"A pretty fantastic kid, one bound to become an awesome adult."

Danny continued to beam. "Mom didn't say much when she'd accidentally busted the music box, but I know she liked it. It was her great-aunt's."

"Then she'll love this gift even more. Other than a puppy for Christmas, would you like anything else?"

Danny shrugged.

He had grabbed a handful of red and green M&M candies

and passed the bowl to Danny. Danny counted aloud ten red ones, then chucked them into his mouth at once.

"You're different from what I thought you'd be," Danny said. "You're cool. And..."

He held his breath.

"Nice. My mom and those kids shouldn't have made fun of you, your family, or your house. Your mother's the coolest teacher I've ever had." Danny picked out three green candies and guzzled them down, making a big production of swirling them around before he swallowed. "And there's something more" he said, with chocolate on his lips.

"Yes?"

"I know my mom's sorry about what she'd done to you when you guys were young. She's been telling me a lot about how wrong she'd been, and how your family is nice. She says she and the other kids were wrong to behave that way. Totally not cool."

"People make mistakes and choose unwisely."

"Yeah, I guess."

He reached for the chocolate sweets. "What counts is the present."

"Like we should be nice to one another? Like God wants us to?"

He silently praised God. "Yes. You got that right."

Danny nodded. "My mom likes you, you know."

"It's important to be good neighbors." He grabbed the pencil and ruler. "Let's scale out our plans."

"I mean she *really* likes you. Get what I mean?"

Visions of Cami had shot before his eyes. Their relationship had been changing. When had the turning point been? The time when Cami and Danny visited at his folks'? Over the spilled popcorn and runaway hamster? The only thing he knew without a doubt was that Cami scored more than simply the "girl next door" when it came to his heart.

He grinned at Danny. "I hear ya. But, hold on. You never answered my question about what you'd like for Christmas."

Danny studied his feet. "Well, like I said at the diner, I want a puppy. Then our dogs can be best pals."

"I'm thinking there's something else you want. Remember, you can trust me, Danny."

"I want my mom to smile again. She hasn't smiled on the inside for a long, long time."

He wanted to ask the boy what would make his mom smile from within, but decided it was best not to delve deeply. His hunch on what would brighten Cami's days was iffy and would take a leap of confidence and faith...

Standing before the bandsaw Gavin thought about what his mom advised before he'd ducked into the shop. He needed to follow his heart.

"Son, you better plan on being less absent-minded when you turn on a piece of equipment like the saw."

Gavin clenched the plans for the music box and turned to face his father.

"Thanks for the reminder, Pop. I'm always careful."

"Your mom told me you were here. She said you were making a gift for your neighbor."

"Pop, her name's Cami."

Jake unbuttoned his jacket. "Spare me useless details I don't want to know."

"That's the trouble. You should know. Cami's a lovely woman, a great mother. She is kind and considerate and—"

"I said, spare me."

"Cami's a totally different adult than the child you once knew. Come on, Pop. You raised five kids. You know too well that children tend to be silly or wild at times. Some are plain mean and wrong." Gavin thumped his chest. "Us kids weren't exactly angelic. You might have polished your resentment for a long time now, but instead of making it shine you're tarnishing it. We're asked to forgive one another and to love one another."

"Cut the preaching. Save it for someone who might benefit from it. I know what's right."

"What's right is to forgive, to love, to move on."

Deep lines grooved his pop's forehead. "What's developing between you and your lady neighbor will only amount to disaster."

Aware he couldn't comfortably assemble it in his father's shop, Gavin stuffed the music box parts back into his coat. But he wouldn't scrap the gift for Cami. He'd hand-cut and fasten it in his own basement if necessary.

"No reply?" A derisive grin spread Pop's lips thin.

"Oh, I have lots to say, but I'm trying my best to respect you. I love you, and deep inside your tough hide I know you love all your kids, including me. In fact, I also know you don't hate others or wish harm to anyone."

"Son, choose."

Choose? Between his family and Cami?

"I said, choose," Pop repeated. "It's her or your family."

He glared at his father. "Pop, this amounts down to one thing. Love. As a child, I'd made a promise to you that as an adult I no longer can honor. Or want to honor."

His father's stone cold expression remained fixed. "Choose."

"I choose to love." Three long strides removed him from the shop. Ten more got him to his car. He'd put his faith in God who will see to his pop's cold, bitter heart. Only He could right this old, festering wrong.

The car seat was ice cold, matching his mood. He inhaled deeply, and the aroma of beef stew wafted straight to his nose. His mouth watered. He jabbed on the dome light. There, in the passenger seat beside him like an old friend, sat a plastic container of his mom's cooking. Beside it sat a plastic container he knew contained the corn bread squares she always fixed with the stew. His emotions smoothed. His mom always amazed him. How different but complementary she was to his father. If God needed to unite his parents, did He also have a plan to reunite him with Cami? Had to be. It was obvious they were more than just neighbors, friends, or an example to others how two people with a sour history could get along.

Gavin started the car. He'd talk with Cami and tell her about how wrong he'd been when he'd promised his father to keep away from her. He also wanted to tell her about the new ultimatum his pop threatened him with, and of the reply he gave.

He'd tell her he loved her.

This truth flooded every pore in his body with warmth that would never turn cold.

"I love you Cami," he tested aloud for the first time. "I love you Cami. I love you."

A glance at the dashboard clock revealed it was past eight. Just maybe she was still awake despite her long workday followed by the stress of Danny's odd, unprecedented behavior.

He floored the gas pedal the few miles home, thankful a police cruiser wasn't hanging around. He hated putting off what could be resolved on a given day. But, his gut tightened when he pulled up to his house and looked across the way. Not a light on. She must have been exhausted and hit the pillow on the early side. No way would he disturb her now.

Well, tomorrow it was, after all. He'd stop by Little Bears, and face-to-face, he'd tell Cami he loved her. Nothing would stop him, not even Danny.

18

"*C*ami, it's no problem having Danny visit on Friday after school. Joey would love to spend time with his pal, and it would give you additional last-minute holiday prep-time."

Cami peered up from the mountain of paperwork on her desk.

Colleen plopped onto the chair beside the desk. "You have that crazed teacher look, like you've stared at homework assignments too long. I bet you haven't heard a word I've said."

She held up her hands. "Guilty."

"What's upsetting you? Let me help."

Cami propped her elbows onto the desk and rubbed at her neck, wondering if the chiropractor had room to fit her in this week. On second thought, make it a massage and she'd be a happy camper.

A massage by Gavin...hmm...he had the hands. She had the aches and pains. He would do wonders for her mind and body. Easily.

Colleen waved a hand in front of Cami's eyes. "You've drifted again. Need some space?"

"Holed up in my office by myself is the last thing I need. Please stay."

"I'm here for you. I have an hour until I'm needed at home."

"Usually I would have to pick Danny up from the community center but my mom's taking him shopping instead. She insists he wears a new dinner jacket for Christmas dinner. It's amazing how she's becoming closer—warmer—since Gavin's entered..."

"Your life?"

Cami straightened and looked at her friend of the past five years. "I take that back. Yes, things have changed since Gavin has re-entered the picture. But, what's making a change for the better is I've allowed God back into my life."

Colleen smiled. "I'm a believer, my friend, and won't argue with you one bit. But I can see the writing on the chalkboard—forgive the wordplay. It doesn't exactly sound as if Gavin Kinkaid is hampering your personal style."

"Ah...well," she said, stretching the words out.

"You're hesitating."

"Life is spurting another mess."

Colleen leaned back into the chair. "Tell me."

She sighed. "There's no ducking out of this, is there?"

"Not from me, there isn't."

"Remember the day of the Open House when you came into this very room and found me a wreck?"

"Well, I wouldn't exactly say that, but yeah, you were upset." Colleen tapped her chin with her index finger. "You were troubled about facing a past with less than stellar memories."

"Understatement." She summarized the childhood conflict with Gavin, his family, and their classmates. "Now you can see this little corner of Pennsylvania hasn't always been serene and charming."

"In one way or the other, we all probably deserve merit badges for surviving childhood. Gavin's different now. And you are as well."

"We've both come long ways, for sure. It's just taken me a little longer to realize this, thanks to a few unexpected road bumps."

"Are you referring to Todd?" Colleen asked gently. "I'm suspecting what happened with your husband helped you to see God's love for you shining bright and strong. Gavin sounds like he embraces the Lord, and based upon your starry-eyed expression I can also see your desire to have him hold onto you. Forever and ever."

She fiddled with a long-ago discarded candy cane shaped pen on the desktop. "There's a problem. Of course."

"Honey, I'm sure you're familiar with the expression 'Nothing that a good miracle can't cure.'"

She accidentally knocked the pen onto the floor. About to pick it up, she froze at the small picture of Jesus she now kept beside a student-decorated pen and pencil canister on the corner of her desk. Colleen was right about miracles.

"Danny is—was—teamed with Gavin at Friends, the group I've mentioned."

"Great program. I'm all ears, continue."

"They were hitting it off well, growing close." She met her friend's gaze. "We were growing close. Colleen, it felt like a little trio of a family was blossoming. You know. Sharing. Laughing. Admitting fears. All that great stuff."

"And a little loving?"

"More like a lot of unexpected loving."

"And you were enjoying it?"

"Every second."

"What happened?"

"Yesterday, Danny arrived home from school upset. He called it quits with Gavin."

"I'm sure it will pass and they'll be on friendly terms again."

"And if it doesn't?" Cami stood, needing to pace.

"You're upset," Colleen reflected, rather than asked. She stepped beside her and gave a hug. "I don't blame you."

"Yeah. You're right. Something wonderful grew between the two of us. I don't know what's going to happen if this simply isn't a passing stage for Danny, like both you and Gavin believe it is. I can't choose between my son and...and a man I..."

"Say it, Cami."

"A man I've fallen in love with," she murmured.

"No," Colleen said softly. "You can't choose. Your son is always first."

"What do I do, then?"

"Pray. God won't misguide your steps." Colleen squeezed her arm. "This just happened yesterday. These things tend to resolve on the pronto side."

"I can only hope."

"God won't let you down. Right?"

"Right."

A knock at the closed office door startled them both. Cami straightened her navy blue blouse and smoothed out her charcoal slacks. She stood straighter, hoping she looked more composed than her frazzled nerves permitted inwardly. "Come in."

Gavin stuck his head in and flashed a winning smile. "Is this a good time for a visit?" He stepped into the office. His black jeans and a tan pullover sweater gave him a sharp, relaxed, and ever-attractive appearance.

"Hi, Gavin," Cami said, a smile tugging at her lips.

Colleen leaned over and whispered into her ear. "Man, oh man, Cami. Go for him!" Aloud, she excused herself and whizzed out of the room.

Cami gripped her collar. This might not be a social visit. "Is something wrong?"

"If you mean with Danny, relax. As far as I know, he's fine. I thought that what I have to say might be best heard in a more private environment." He glanced about the room. "Like here, in your office."

"You mean, away from Danny." She nervously chuckled, but it came out like a groan.

"Am I obvious?"

"Yep. I can't blame you, though. Not after the way my son treated you yesterday. Again, I apologize for his behavior."

He eyed the chair where Colleen had sat. "May I have a seat? I didn't get much sleep last night and truthfully, I'm beat."

"Where are my manners? And here I'm talking about my son's." She gestured for him to have a seat. About to walk around to her desk, he grasped her wrist.

Her pulse jumped beneath the gentle touch of his fingertips. Slowly, he slid his warm hand to her icy fingertips. Her breath eased, a recurrent reaction around him.

He closed the distance between them tighter. "Cami, sweetheart, I've been thinking about you the whole day."

She sat down behind her desk and gestured again for him to have a seat. He pulled the vacant chair mere inches to her side.

"I'll try not to keep you long," he added.

"Time isn't an issue. My mom has Danny until dinnertime."

He arched a brow. "Sounds like things are smoothing out between your family. How's Theresa feeling?"

"Much better, thanks for asking. She's taking her new medication as prescribed and admits it's helping. And, you're right—a change has occurred among us. A positive one."

His smile faded. He dragged his hands down his face.

"I hope I haven't misspoken."

"No, not at all. Your news is actually good. Make that great."

"I can see something's weighing you down. Is it more than Danny?"

He pulled back. "When we were kids my sisters and I made a promise to Pop. I'm not proud of what I vowed."

Ah, this is what his sister Donna confessed in confidence. Cami waited patiently for him to continue.

"Pop's a funny guy. Sometimes, he could be the best pal a son could ever wish for. Other times, he could be unrelentingly cold and stubborn, someone you want to distant yourself from."

"Is that why you took off after graduation?"

"You have amazing, calm eyes. When I'm with you, Cami, it's difficult to become tense. I don't want to upset you talking about family troubles or other past problems."

She leaned back into her chair, hoping her casual body language would relax him further. "But you need to tell me something important."

He nodded. "Pop asked me and my sisters to keep a separate life from you and the other kids who caused trouble. Not out of revenge, though. Jake Kinkaid isn't a revengeful man. Or one to fight back, physically. I think it was more his way of coping, trying to protect his family without further giving the town news to think about." He leaned over his knees and rubbed between his eyes.

"I understand."

"There's more. My sisters don't know everything."

What had Donna left out?

"As the only boy, I felt as if I'd been thrown into a corner with no way out. I've always believed in God. On one hand I wanted not to seek revenge and to honor Pop." He rubbed at the back of his neck. "On the other hand, it left me stripped of the power to speak up in defense of my family. This inability to support my parents and sisters on the public level made me feel like I've done more of a disservice to them than good. Not good for the only son in the family."

"And you keeping your distance from them these past few years only made these feelings grow more sour?"

"Made me feel like a total loser. The more confused I became the more I stayed away. And the more my regret deepened. A vicious cycle."

"I understand where you're coming from. I'm sorry you carried such a burden." She stepped to the window. The snow-covered playground, a solitary chickadee, and a woman jogging behind a baby stroller colored the world simple and pristine. She shook her head. Life was complicated. Yet, she refused to view herself as helpless to brighten her own little world. No way would she throw away her passions to enjoy life or to help her son reach for the most life can give him and to teach him to give back to others.

Then again, a man and a woman who loved each other could certainly create a blissful union. They could make a needed sanctuary from life's storms.

She looked at Gavin. Could they, united, create this badly needed haven?

"Cami," he said softly, standing beside her. "I'm here to talk about us, not my family."

"Us?"

He nodded. "Looking back, it's no surprise how those times drew me closer to God. I couldn't do it myself. I gave it all to Him, telling Him I couldn't handle the messes in my life. I stepped back. God stepped forward. Today, other than those unpleasant memories, I'm thankful nothing remains in this town to show for that relatively minuscule time in history. I want to keep all that in the past, and hope you do too, honey."

She wanted to be strong and brave. For Gavin. For herself. For Danny. Against her will, tears shimmied down her cheeks. He brushed them away gently. Without a word, he turned her around and pulled her protectively against his chest, his immediate warmth a shield against the scary uncertainties in life.

"Ah, Cami. Cami. Everything about you is sweet."

She eased back only enough to peer into his eyes. "You were so brave back then; still are. I can't imagine Danny going through that chaos and pressure and pray he never will."

"No, I wasn't brave."

Her brows pinched. "But you just said—"

"That I let God take care of things. I do now, but until recently,

I resented the past and carried a chip on my shoulders. Big shoulders, big chip. I tried to handle things myself, but ended up pretty miserable instead."

"What changed?"

He pulled her closer, brushing his lips tenderly over hers.

"Meeting you again."

"I don't understand."

"I regret the past troubles that occurred between us. But, I have no regrets about what else had occurred. I've embraced God more fully and saw how I could use this whole experience to help others. Honey, it also brought us together again. These are the only things that count."

All breath escaped Cami. Her jaw went slack. Gavin traced his fingertips across her lips. Adoration beamed from his eyes.

"No regrets," she finally said, in a murmur barely recognizable to her own ears.

"No regrets."

Fresh tears escaped from her eyes. Again, he wiped them.

Did she deserve this man? She blinked another round of tears. No, love wasn't dependent upon deserving. That's what Gavin had shown her every day since they'd met again when he'd first looked at the house across the street. Daily since their reunion two months ago, he reminded her there was no earning this beautiful thing called love. Love was a gift, free and priceless.

"There's one more thing."

She lifted her gaze to his beautiful blue-gray eyes. She saw tranquility and assurance.

"Pop and I rumbled through a one-on-one last night."

She tensed.

"It's okay." He braced her upper arms. "God doesn't lead us to a certain place and then abandon us."

"What happened between you two?"

A rap came at the office door.

"May I come in?"

She stiffened at her friend's strained tone. "What is it, Colleen?"

"Danny's teacher is on the main line for you."

"Mrs. Kinkaid?" Without waiting for a reply Cami bolted to her desk and pressed the main line.

"Hello. This is Cami Richardson." She heard the words she wished she'd mistaken. In need of physical support, she leaned against the desk. "I'll be right there," she replied, unable to keep the shock and shakiness from her voice.

She turned to see the man she loved and her close friend standing nearby. Concern etched both of their faces. She rushed the words out, but knew it wouldn't hasten a resolution, let alone an explanation.

"Danny's been caught hurling a brick through one of your folks' windows. Your mom managed to separate Jake and Danny from a tangle, but urged me to get over there quickly. She fears the worst will erupt any second."

19

*C*ami searched the four pairs of eyes of those seated around Beth Kinkaid's kitchen table. In addition to Danny, Gavin, and herself, there was Beth and Cami's mom. Jake stood off to the side. But, it was Danny's pale and drawn face that told her all she needed to know. Her son was innocent. And he was petrified over the consequences.

"I want him out of this house," Jake demanded, his voice gravelly. Contempt wrinkled his face. He leaned against the sink and folded his arms.

"Give us a chance, Jake," Beth said evenly to her husband. She faced Danny. "Danny, my husband says he witnessed you breaking one of our windows. You say you didn't. With your mom here, please tell us again what happened."

"It doesn't matter that Mom is here, Mrs. Kinkaid." Danny stared at an unknown speck on the table. "I didn't do it."

From the corner of her eye, Cami saw Jake bristle. She pulled her attention back to her son. Jake could take his intimidation elsewhere. She needed to be strong for Danny.

"Sweetie," she said softly. "Would it be easier for you to tell me details if it were just us two in the room?"

Danny shook his head. "No, Mom. I'd only say the same thing 'cause that's the truth. I don't lie."

"I know, bud. You always tell me the truth and I have no reason to think otherwise when it comes to other folks. But, the Kinkaids have broken glass on their carpet. They're trying to understand what happened."

"Then they'll have to try harder," Danny snapped.

"Good thing he's not my kid," Jake said. "I'd take soap to his mouth lightning fast. He wouldn't see it coming."

"My grandson is not your son," Theresa said. "And that's obviously a good thing."

Gavin leaned back from the table, his mouth twisted to one side. "Pop, I wouldn't go making this more difficult for Danny. Or anyone."

"Son, don't tell me how to live in my house. There are no excuses. I pulled into the driveway just in time to see a brick flying through the air, to watch it hit our front window, to hear glass shatter, and then saw this punk kid with a second brick in his hand who is now sitting in my own kitchen and denying everything." Jake leveled a glare at his son. "Sad you're doubting your own father."

Beth shushed them both. "This is no time for a world war, let alone family strife. Cool it, you two." She looked at Cami, anticipation brimming her eyes.

"Once more, Danny," Cami said. She rubbed his back. "Tell me again what happened."

Danny wriggled free from her touch. "Ethan and I were walking after school. I know I was supposed to wait for Grandma, but Ethan told me he wanted to show me something. When we got here, he dared me to throw a brick like when..." He gulped hard. "Like..."

"Go on," she coaxed.

"It's not good, Mom. Ethan wanted me to throw the brick like his dad once did when he was a kid—right through the same window his dad bragged about doing." Danny dropped his gaze to his lap. "Ethan said his dad went off about how all the kids did this stuff to the Kinkaids. And said that it would be a cool thing to do since our parents did it too. But I told him no way. So he threw the brick."

Jake pounded his fist on the countertop. A cup in the dish rack rattled. He turned toward the window. Gavin, seated between his mom and Cami, placed a hand on both of their shoulders.

"I told Ethan he was mean and wrong," Danny continued. "I told him he had no business throwing the brick at the Kinkaid's house—or anyone's house. Ethan told me I was stupid, and shoved another brick in my hand. He dared me to throw this one through another window. That's when Mr. Kinkaid came home and Ethan ran off before Mr. Kinkaid got out of his car. And that's why I had the brick in my hand. Wish I never met up with that troublemaker."

"Yeah, right," Jake said. "Totally innocent. Like I haven't heard this before."

"Please, let's give the child a chance to explain," Beth said.

Jake frowned. "He's explained it all. It's a bunch of neat and tidy fabrications."

Gavin moved beside his father. Jake sidestepped away.

"Pop, be reasonable. Let's—"

"Oh, I'm being reasonable, son." Jake swiped the room with a pointed finger. "You're forgetting who the culprit is and who the victim is. A man has to watch over his family. I've already said this once, but I'll say it again: I want this boy out of my house. No delay. I get to make the rules under this roof."

"Pop, be fair."

Jake stared at Gavin. "Like I said in the shop last night, make a choice. Your family or the neighbor woman and her worthless boy."

Cami stood. "Mr. Kinkaid, I understand your problem with

me, and how you're upset about the broken window, but it's a sorry world when adults believe children are worthless."

"No," Danny yelled. He pushed back his chair; it toppled to the floor. The room knifed into silence as he ran out the side door.

Jake snorted. "The guilty always flee."

Gavin retrieved his car keys from his pant pockets. "Let's go, Cami."

Theresa stood. "I'm leaving too."

"Gavin, are you siding with the brat's mother?" Jake asked.

"Danny is not a brat. No child is." He narrowed his eyes at his father. "Cami and I are neighbors. We came in one car—mine. It's winter. I'm not making them walk home."

Jake shoved his hands into his front pants pockets. "Then what are you going to do, son?"

Gavin stopped at the door. "What I always do when I need guidance—pray."

Jake turned his back.

"Cami," Gavin said. "Ready to leave?"

She nodded, but held her ground. She took one step toward Jake. "And I'm praying too that our Father's peace soothes your heart."

She ignored the buttons on her coat and pulled the garment tighter around her middle, wishing it were a pair of comforting arms instead. Prior to meeting up with Gavin a few months ago, she'd forgotten God's love and power, setting His ways aside. Gavin helped to guide her back to God's unconditional love. This was no time to stop trusting Him. The outcome would turn out to be right since God was never wrong.

As they approached the car she could see Danny already sitting in the backseat. It would be a long, silent ride home.

20

*T*hursday whipped by. Then Friday. Two more days left until Christmas.

Cami shoved her mug of cold coffee away from her untouched breakfast of wheat toast and fig spread. For a holiday season of joy, peace, and good will, a gut-wrenching despondency declared itself a new resident under her roof.

"Why?" Her own spoken word startled her. Although she hadn't shouted the word, she glanced around the kitchen, half-expecting a sleepy-eyed Danny to plod in and ask what the commotion was about.

No Danny. She looked at the rustic apple-shaped clock over the kitchen sink. Eight-thirty. Her baby had slept late this morning. Understandably, he'd been withdrawn since their meeting with the Kinkaids. Extra sleep might bring him a little comfort.

She bowed her head in prayer. "Father, I pray for your blessings. Danny wouldn't hurt anyone. He embraces you. I confess, sometimes, he embraces you more than I do. He's a good boy. Please have mercy on him. Amen."

The oven timer dinged.

She pulled out two trays of raspberry jam-filled thumbprint

cookies on a trivet to cool, breathing in the sweet sugar and buttery aroma steaming from the pans. Her gaze drifted out the window to the snow-covered walkway that led to the road and easily across the street to Gavin's house. She wondered if he'd been busy these past few days with holiday preparation and family get-togethers, though she had difficulty imagining that latter when it came to Jake, especially after their fiasco meeting over the brick-throwing. Since that day Gavin hadn't phoned nor knocked at her door. Then again, she hadn't made a first-step approach either. It was as if they've been complete strangers these past few months. Worst, it was as if love never existed between them. And this was love, for sure. Not a crush. Nor infatuation, nor daydream.

The living room's mantle clock chimed. The singsong pings echoed down the hallway and into the kitchen. Nine o'clock. Danny still hadn't come downstairs.

Her arms prickled with gooseflesh. No. Oh, no. Couldn't be.

She headed for the stairs. Walk slowly and calmly. Everything is fine. Yeah, right. She pounded the steps at full gallop.

"Danny?" She entered his bedroom. "It's time to start the day, sleepyhead." She stepped to his bed and knew instantly there was a problem. A major one. No Danny. Only ruffled sheets and two pillows shoved under the blankets to give an illusion of a sleeping child.

She bolted down the stairs. Her knotted belly told her she wouldn't find her son anywhere in the house. Not bothering to don a coat, she fled outdoors and into the backyard.

"Danny," she yelled. "It's okay, my sweet peppermint. Come out." Silly words. Danny never pulled pranks. He wouldn't be hiding from her.

She raced around the house in hope to fine Danny building a snow fort or rolling a snowball. Instead, she caught Gavin stepping onto his front steps. Dressed in disheveled jeans and a black T-shirt, he looked as if sleep had eluded him for days. Their gazes locked. He rocked back on his heels. A look of concern draped over him. He opened his mouth to...offer comfort? To reveal Danny's whereabouts?

"Hey, Mom."

She whirled around. Danny rushed to her side.

"You look worried, Mom."

"It's not everyday I discover my son missing."

"Oh, Mom."

Patience. Learn. Love. Don't jump on the child.

She pulled him into a fierce embrace, not caring if it embarrassed him. "I'm glad you're back and aren't hurt. Let's talk."

"I guess." Danny glanced across the way toward Gavin's, but he was gone. He must have stepped indoors. Danny stared at the ground. "Can we go inside?"

She led her son straight to the sofa. "Please, buddy, spill it. Tell me everything. I love you, Danny. I want to know where you've been and why."

He kicked off his sneakers, leaned back into the soft, cushiony back and drew his knees to his chest. "I took a walk."

"Go anywhere in particular?"

He shrugged.

She toed her shoes off, leaned back beside her son, and raised her knees too. And waited in silence. Her little boy had her love, and all of the time he needed to share whatever he wanted.

Danny rubbed at his knees. "Mom, if we're supposed to love one anther, how come we don't? How come God made it hard when He wants us to love so badly?"

She wrapped an arm around Danny. "I think it's not that God has made it difficult for us to love one another, but we people have made it difficult for ourselves. God doesn't ask us to do things we're unable to do. And love is one of those things."

He nodded into her side.

"Were you thinking about this earlier when you went for a walk?"

"Sort of." He sat straighter, lowering his legs to the floor. "I went to talk to Mr. Kinkaid."

She swallowed hard. "You're no longer calling him Gavin?"

Danny scrunched his face. "Not that Mr. Kinkaid. I meant Gavin's dad."

She visualized Danny walking one too many blocks, alone, to the Kinkaid's home at the southern tip of the lake, nearly across town. The last she'd looked at the outdoor thermometer it read a crisp twenty degrees. "Oh, my. It's freezing outside. I could have driven you over."

"I'm a big boy, Mom. I had big boy things to do."

She nodded, shoving aside for a future time the needed conversation about safety and taking off at the tender age of eight. "What happened between you two?"

"I knocked at the door. Mrs. Kinkaid answered. She said she wasn't surprised to see me and took me to Mr. Kinkaid who was fixing something in his shop." He fingered the fringes on the red and green Christmas throw draped over the sofa's arm.

"Go on, love."

"I told him the same exact thing that I said when we were all there the other day. I also said something I haven't told you yet, or anyone."

She gently massaged Danny's back.

"Ethan threatened me, Mom. He also threatened to hurt you and Gavin or anyone I love."

She stiffened, but Danny continued before she could say a word more.

"Ethan's been saying for the longest of times that Gavin is bad news. That's when I got confused and didn't know how to act or think around Gavin. I think I messed things up between us. But then Ethan told me he'd hurt both you and Gavin if I didn't help break a window at the Kinkaid's house. I told Mr. Kinkaid I only was there pretend-like so I could stop Ethan, but it didn't work out that way. Do you believe me?"

"Of course I believe you." She wiped a runaway tear from her brave son with her fingertips. She smiled. "I believe you did exactly what God would have wanted you to do. I'm proud of you."

Danny sniffled loudly. "Yeah?"

"Definitely. Tell me what Mr. Kinkaid said."

"That he'd have to think about it. I offered to pay for the window with my allowance money, but he said that wasn't necessary."

She held back a grin. "Mr. Kinkaid will come to accept what you're saying as the truth. I can talk with Ethan's parents, if you'd like. I don't think they'd be pleased to learn of their son's mean-spirited behavior."

Danny nodded. "Okay."

"Does this mean you're not upset with Gavin?"

"No, I like him. A lot. He's a great guy. I was trying to watch out for him. But now he must think I hate him and his family."

"For starters, let's phone Gavin. We can invite him over and explain everything. Deal?"

Danny smiled. "Deal."

But, Gavin wasn't home.

Nor would he answer any of the messages Cami left.

21

*P*arked in the church's lot, Cami flashed on the dome light to check whether Danny's tie was straight. He complained, again, how he didn't like to wear the silly, tight thing around his neck despite its theme of decorated Christmas trees. She offered a smile, no reprimands. Her poor baby already suffered from not being able to make amends with Gavin, and from not knowing yet if Jake would accept his peace offering.

She glanced at the clock on the dashboard. "My goodness. We're five minutes late for the service. Let's hurry."

Gavin's mom, his four sisters and their families were stretched across two middle pews. Everyone but Gavin and his dad were there. Beth stood upon seeing Cami and Danny. She motioned for them to join her family. Beth whispered, "You have a wonderful son. I think he's helping to bring Jake back to church."

Cami looked around, confused.

Beth leaned toward her. "He'll be here. You'll see."

Cami smiled and turned to help her son slip out from his blue parka. She leaned toward his ear while pointing to the crèche in front of the altar. "God gave us a gift-wrapped present—"

"Baby Jesus," Danny whispered back, awe in his voice, a smile lighting his face.

"Yes. He came wrapped in God's love for each of us."

"Because God loves us, right?"

"Yes, He does." Cami repeated this belief to herself, trying to push aside the hurt over the inability to talk with Gavin the past few days. She too needed to focus on the meaning of Christmas.

The choir began a favorite hymn and she hummed quietly. She watched a few latecomers scramble to the last few available pews. No Gavin, nor his dad. The seats they'd saved for them seemed to have tripled in size.

Her heart tightened.

The choir began singing the last verse. Distantly, she heard the rustling of additional people. As she tried to concentrate solely on the hymn, Gavin and Jake slipped beside her. Her mom and dad followed.

Joy and hope surged throughout her. She scooted over allowing room for Jake to sit with his wife. The tall, once surly man stepped beside Danny and pulled him into a bear hug, patting the boy's back. He then slipped by and joined Beth. Gavin sat to Danny's right and stretched his arm around Danny, touching Cami's shoulder. She peered at him curiously.

"I've been praying," he mouthed.

She nodded. "Me too."

At midnight, the congregation stood and welcomed in Christmas with praise and song. While hugs and greetings were shared and excited children urged their folks to hurry them home to see what Santa had tucked under the trees, Cami beamed at her and Gavin's united families. One by one she pulled each into a hug and thanked them for coming to church and being there for God, Gavin, and her.

With Gavin's return, Cami held fast to the conviction God wouldn't bring them to this juncture in life only to separate them again. She loved how God always gently put her back on course. She loved God. She loved Gavin. Somehow, it would work out.

She laced her fingers with Gavin's. "Will you come over tonight for a few minutes?"

He smiled; his eyes twinkled. "Yes. I would have invited myself if you hadn't asked. There's a little something I have for Danny and you."

She grasped his shirt collar, loving every second of holding onto him. "But I don't have a gift for you."

"I'm thinking you might."

About to question him, he murmured he'd meet her back at her place.

Thirty minutes later she opened her front door to welcome Gavin. Still dressed in her church clothes, but now with feet comfy warm in her fuzzy penguin slippers, she stood confident that this wonderful man would view her as fine no matter what she wore. And she would think the same of him. A man of his word, he'd come home to her.

Danny sailed into Gavin's waiting arms. "I'm sorry about everything."

"I know you are, chief. Pop told me about what you shared with him. You're the greatest kid ever, Danny. Thank you for standing up for us. I love you, kiddo."

Danny stepped back. "Cool. I love you too." He tugged at Gavin's arm. "Come inside and check out our tree."

"One sec." Gavin stepped to the door and swept Cami into his arms, kissing her with unmistakable passion that warmed her from head to toe.

Danny raised his arm in cheer. "Does this mean you love my mom?"

Gavin pulled back from Cami only enough to look her in the eye. "Does it ever." He reached out the door and carried in a medium sized bag. "What's Christmas without gifts?"

Danny whooped. "Yay."

"Oh, Gavin," Cami said. "All I can offer you are Christmas cookies."

He grinned wide. "Oh, no. There's a lot more."

They settled around the Christmas tree tucked in the living room corner.

"First," Gavin said, "Danny and I have a gift for you, Cami."

Danny's brows lifted. "We do?"

He whispered into Danny's ears.

"Oh, right. We do have a present for you, Mom."

Gavin handed Danny a gift-wrapped present and nudged him to give it to his mom.

She rubbed her hands together. "I can't imagine."

"Open it, Mom," Danny said.

The shiny red paper unfolded to white tissue paper that unfolded to...

"Oh wow," she shrieked.

"Why are you crying, Mom? You don't like it?"

She stared at the beautifully crafted music box, a perfect match to her Auntie Fran's, the one she'd dropped and broken the evening she'd first seen Gavin after many years of separation.

"I *love* it, Danny." She kissed her son then Gavin. "When did you guys make this?"

"Let's just say God has an interesting way of working." Gavin faced Danny. "I have a present for you, too. I'll bring it over tomorrow, if your mom allows and if you promise to take care of it."

"You bet I will."

"It's not a puppy like Happy, but my friend has to move to a place where pets aren't allowed and he has a one-year-old cat." Gavin glanced at Cami. "Clyde is box-trained and loves children and scratching posts."

Danny's eyes widened. "Can we keep Clyde, Mom?"

She couldn't refuse a gift from Gavin, this extraordinary man

God had gifted her with. "Sure." She stood, watching Danny beam.

Gavin looked longingly into her eyes. "And where do you think you're going? I'm not quite finished."

"To get the cookies."

"They can wait. It's your turn."

"Mine?" she mouthed and sank back into her seat. From the glittering tree lights, Gavin looked as if *he* were her present. "You guys just gave me the most precious gift."

"Cami, sweetheart." He withdrew a midnight-black box from his shirt pocket and opened the box.

She could barely see the sparkling diamond for the tears blurring her vision.

"Oh, there she goes," Danny said. "Crying, again."

"Joyfully," she said, her breath choppy. "This is no *little* gift, Gavin."

He slid the ring onto her finger. "Marry me, Cami. I love you so much, honey. I always want to be by your side." He looked lovingly at Danny. "And I want Danny to be my son."

She threw herself into his arms. Together, they pulled Danny into their embrace.

"Yes, I'll marry you, Gavin. I love you. I know we're meant to be with each other for the rest of our lives."

He kissed the tears from her cheeks, his lips warm and luscious.

Her heart glowed, and filled her with a peace she knew was here to stay. "I'd wondered what God had up His sleeve the day you moved across the way. Our love will free us from the hurts we've fostered long enough."

"Yes, I agree. We'll finally be able to have a future instead of worrying about what happened in the past. However, right now, I have something better in mind." He feathered his fingers across her face and pressed his lips to hers.

In the back of her mind Cami realized Danny had left the room. Probably for his bed, to dream sweet dreams.

"Your house or mine?" he asked when they pulled back from each other. "Nah. Answer later." He pulled her into another delicious kiss.

Moments, or perhaps an eternity later, they sat on the floor. With their backs against the sofa, in the sparkling lights of the Christmas tree, Cami leaned her head against Gavin's chest. "I'm madly in love with you. Anywhere with you is the best place to live because we'll be safe and secure with God's love for us."

"Did you see the inscription on the back of the music box?"

"No." She swooped up the gift and examined it more carefully. On its back she found a brass plate. "Christmas is forever at Kindred Lake."

"That's the only thing that counts when I have you and Danny in my life."

Still holding the music box, she shared a kiss he wouldn't soon forget.

When they pulled away, she sprang onto her feet. "Do you hear what I hear?"

He cupped his ear. "Music from the string quartet."

"Yes." She wound the key on the music box to release the music. Then, she pulled the love of her life into a hug. "Will you dance with me, Gavin?"

"For always and always. Know why?"

"In addition to us wonderfully in love with each other?"

He stroked her cheek, his warm fingers playing its own melody across her skin. "It might have taken a while, but we've truly made amends into amens. " His eyes twinkled. He pressed her lips with a long kiss until they both moaned. When they parted, he said, "And we finally figured out this thing called love."

"Love never arrives late," she said and wrapped her arms around him, never wanting to let go.

ACKNOWLEDGMENTS

Gratitude and love to:

My forever always companion, my Lord and Savior, Jesus Christ.

My dear friends and wonderful authors Kathleen Rouser and Megan Whitson Lee. Heartfelt thanks for your encouragement, hand-holding, and advice.

My Avenue E Street Team cheering squad, you ladies are the sweetest and most supportive.

The winner of my Author Newsletter Contest, Caryl Kane, thanks for the cutest and most appropriate name of *Happy* for Gavin's dog. So glad you shared your memories of your own Happy!

ABOUT THE AUTHOR

Elaine Stock is the author of the novel *Her Good Girl*, winner of the 2018 American Fiction Awards in the Christian Inspirational category, and *Always With You*, which won the 2017 Christian Small Publishers Association Book of the Year Award in fiction. *And You Came Along*, a novella, released in December 2017. Her novels fuse romance, family drama and faith in a clean fiction style. She is a member of American Christian Fiction Writers, Romance Writers of America, and Women's Fiction Writers Association. In addition to Twitter, Facebook, and Goodreads, she hangs out on her active blog, Everyone's Story, dedicated to uplifting and encouraging all readers through the power of story and hope.

Born in Brooklyn, NY, Elaine has now been living in upstate, rural New York with her husband for more years than her stint as a NYC gal. She enjoys long walks down country roads, visiting New England towns, and of course, a good book.

Please visit Elaine at: http://elainestock.com

facebook.com/AuthorElaineStock

twitter.com/ElaineStock

goodreads.com/ElaineStock

ALSO BY ELAINE STOCK

Always With You: Winner of the 2017 Christian Small Publisher Book of the Year Award in fiction, a tale of falling in love with a man you were warned to stay away from.

Amazon: http://amzn.to/21uGtGF

Barnes and Noble: http://bit.ly/1PfRyXX

Her Good Girl: Winner of the 2018 American Fiction Awards in Christian inspirational fiction, the story of what happens to a family when the hurt gets so bad that an outsider decides to take things into his own hands and it may not be for the better.

Amazon: http://amzn.to/2loWMxM

And You Came Along: A companion novella to *Christmas Love Year Round*. Is true love ever mistaken?

Amazon: http://amzn.to/2jyBMwK

Barnes and Noble: http://bit.ly/2AKXKHR

Look for Book Two and Book Three of the Kindred Lake Series:

Book Two *When Love Blossoms*

Book Three *The Colors of Love*